The Cowboy Kid

By Shawn Howell & J.R. Blomberg

Chapter 1

1946.

Emmie Murray stepped onto the porch as
the sun began to chin itself on the Big Horn
Mountains. A few strands of her brunette hair,
tied up, had found their way to freedom,
falling on her shoulders. This wild and
beautiful country of northern Wyoming had
always been home and the cool stillness of the
new day always put her mind at ease. Being
eight months pregnant, it came in handy today

because stomach pains had kept her from having a decent night's sleep.

On clear mornings, like this one, Emmie felt a shiver run through her as she reminded herself this really is her life. The rippling grasses and sound of the streams were familiar but it always surprised her that she still looked at it like it was the first time. At only twenty six, her and her husband, two years her senior, are the youngest ranchers in the valley and it was not an opportunity to be taken for granted.

Ranching is hard work, but no one was more willing to carve out their place in the world than Sam and Emmie. Their small one story house had been fixed up, with Sam adding the porch she was standing on. The barn was freshly painted and the overhang where their 1944 Ford pickup truck is parked had gotten a new roof this year. The small improvements made it feel like home.

Emmie's reminiscing of the months of work is interrupted by the sound of hooves. With a smile on her face, she turns to see a herd of ten horses cresting over a grass covered hill. The running animals churn up the earth as they descend the small mound. On horseback, pushing the herd from behind, is Sam Murray.

Emmie's smile is matched by Sam's as he runs the horses towards the barn and into a large holding pen. His blue eyes catch Emmie waving as the animals rumble past. Sam, with his square jaw, acknowledges her with a nod of his head and continues to push the horses into the arena. With the last horse through the gate, Sam rides up and closes it. Reaching down, he stroked his horse's neck as he turned him towards the ranch house.

Emmie, leaning on the porch rail, watched Sam ride his horse right to the steps of the porch and pull rein.

"Well, Mrs. Murray, I would say this is our best group yet."

"I never get tired of watching you ride up to this house," Emmie said.

Sam gets off his horse and ties the reins to the porch rail. He walks up the steps and removes his black felt cowboy hat, revealing his ash blond hair, as he leans down to kiss her. This move never fails to impress Emmie.

"And how's little Kade?" Sam asked, rubbing Emmie's stomach.

"Or Kaddie. Just like you, wants the job done before it even starts," Emmie said.

Sam has always admired Emmie's open mindedness, but he can't escape the feeling of having a son. He gives her a sly grin while looking into her eyes.

5

"How about a cup of coffee?" Emmie said.

"Beautiful and a mind reader. I don't know how I got to be so lucky," Sam said.

Emmie returns Sam's grin with one of her own as she steps ahead of him and opens the front door, entering their house. Sam knocks some dust off his hat and walks over to a pair of wooden chairs flanking a small table. After a quick look at his horse, Sam takes a seat and puts his hat on the table.

Emmie, cups of coffee in hand, backs through the front door. She approaches Sam and gives him one of the mugs.

"Thank you," Sam said, sipping the coffee. "Despite what some people say, you do make a great cup of coffee."

Emmie sits down next to Sam, not amused with his back handed compliment.

"Same people told me to stay away from you," Emmie said, watching Sam take another sip of coffee, his eyes looking over the cup at her, "but they were wrong."

"The place is really starting to come together," Sam said after a deep breath. Looking at Emmie, he takes her hand. "Little Kade…"

"Or Kaddie," Emmie interjects again.

"…is going to make the place a home." Sam said.

"You are a man of your word," Emmie said, placing her other hand on top of Sam's. "Our baby is lucky you are going to be his, or her, father. With that in mind, let's finish up so we're not-late."

"Late?" Sam said confused.

"Sam! You promised me. Did you already forget?" Emmie said.

"Forget?" Sam said, desperately trying to remember. "No, I didn't forget."

"You did," Emmie said noticing the searching look in Sam's eyes. "We're going to church today." Sam sips his coffee with a sigh, thinking of the work he could get done instead of wasting time at church. "This is not for you. It's for our family."

"Yes, Ma'am." Sam said.

Chapter 2

The Sheridan County Church sits off a
dirt highway nestled in between two large
trees. The white "A" framed building, with a
small steeple on the roof, stands out in the
mid morning sun. Standing in the parking lot,
which is mixed with pickup trucks, cars, and
even a tractor, hymns can be heard from
within.

It's standing room only inside the little
church. The Preacher standing in front of the
congregation is an older gentleman with white

hair. The faces looking back at him are from all walks of life, but all are distinctly Big Horn Country. The farmers and ranchers, the miner's and oil field workers, the folks from town; everyone wearing their Sunday best.

Sam and Emmie sit in the second row. She is holding *The Bible* for the two of them and helping Sam follow along. Emmie sings right along with the hymn as Sam hums and follows her finger on the page. Sam is uncomfortable and keeps fussing with his neck-tie.

When the collection plate makes its way to Sam, he stops fussing with his clothes and stares at it. With a nudge from Emmie, he pulls a quarter out of his pocket and places it in the collection plate. The disappointed look on Emmie's face keeps Sam from passing the plate on. With an exhale, Sam digs back into his pocket and places a one dollar bill. With a reassuring smile from his wife, Sam

passes the collection plate to the next
parishioner.

With the sermon over, the parishioners
are filing out of the church and waiting to
shake hands with the preacher. Sam and Emmie
are next in line and the Preacher smiles as
Emmie walks up.

"Hello, Emmie" the pastor greets her
warmly.

"Pastor, always nice to see you," Emmie
said as she gestures towards Sam. "I would
like you to meet my husband, Sam."

"Very nice to meet you." The pastor
nodded as Sam tips his hat. "It always fills
my heart to see new faces joining us."

"It was a lovely sermon," Emmie said.

"I am so glad you enjoyed it." The
Preacher glanced down at Emmie's pregnant
belly. "Faith is the back-bone of all

families," he commented, looking Sam right in the eye. "Your own and the Lord's."

Sam nods his head and shakes the pastor's hand. Emmie gives him a quick hug.

"I hope we will see you again," he said, looking at Sam.

"Yes, of course," Sam said, avoiding the stern glare coming from his wife.

"Wonderful," said the pastor, concluding the exchange.

Sam and Emmie make their way down the church steps to find fellow ranch owners, Paul and Judy Peterson. They are talking with a couple the Murrays do not know.

"Sam Murray, you lost?" Paul calls as he notices Sam walking down the church steps.

"Paul, Judy," Sam says as he tips his hat and they join the group. Sam and Paul shake hands.

"Hello, Emmie," Paul said heartily, hugging against his tall and slender frame. "You remember my wife, Judy."

"Yes, of course. Hello, Judy," Emmie smiled.

"Always a pleasure to see you, Emmie," Judy said as she gestures towards the couple that the Murrays don't know. "Have you met Barbara and John Howard? They just took over the general store in town."

"No. Very nice to meet you both," she said, extending hand.

With three couples, it does not take long for the men to break off into their own conversation, leaving the women to keep chatting.

"Sam, how's the new place treating you?" Paul said while running his fingers through his crisp mustache.

"We're getting along. Just this morning I was telling Emmie how it's starting to come together," Sam said.

"That's good to hear. It does take time," Paul said.

"Yeah, one day we'll give the Bar P a run for its' money," Sam said.

"I have no doubt. But listen if you need any help let me know," Paul said.

"I appreciate that," Sam said.

"Remember I can always use some good horses. I know you're starting with solid bloodlines." Paul said.

"With a little time, I can make that happen." Sam said. Turning to the shorter and balding man, he asks, "John, you a rancher too?"

"No, I prefer the comforts of town." John said, making the men laugh.

Sam looks over his shoulder to make sure Emmie is fine. Her smile gives him the answer he is looking for and he turns his attention back to the men. Emmie listens to what Judy Peterson has to say.

"You know Emmie, Barbara just had a little girl," Judy said.

"Sarah's almost one now. It goes by so fast. How far along are you?" Barbara said, looking at Emmie's stomach.

"Eight months yesterday," Emmie replies, smiling.

"How are you feeling?" Barbara asks.

"So far, so good. A little nervous about delivering " Emmie said.

"It's always like that with your first," Barbara said. "Sarah was our first. It's the hardest and most important experience of your life."

"My husband and I are looking forward to it." Emmie said.

"I hope a safe and speedy delivery on the blessed new bundle," Barbara said.

Chapter 3

The late afternoon breeze blows across the Murray ranch, slightly moving the tail of a grazing bay horse. It's no reason to get spooked because all the livestock know it's the beginning of the end of another day but something has the horse on alert. Ears pricked, head now high, the horse cranes its neck to check the surroundings.

Riding through the tall grass, at a walk, are Sam and Emmie. The bay horse turns and trots over to its herd mates as the couple makes their way through the pasture.

"God this place is so beautiful," Emmie said. "Thank you for today."

Looking at Emmie, Sam said, "No, thank you honey."

"Our child is going to be so blessed to have two great men in their life," Emmie said.

"Two?"

"You and my father…" said Emmie, exasperation evident in her voice.

At the sound of the word 'father,' Sam subtly cringed. It's a knee jerk reaction he stops quickly for the sake of avoiding another argument.

"I don't know about all that, but he will have the best mother," Sam said.

"You're a good man. Thank you for making me feel special. I love you," Emmie said looking into Sam's eyes as he blushes.

"I love you too," Sam replies.

"How was Paul?" Emmie asks.

"Good. He's looking to get three or four horses from us." Sam said.

"Like you said, it's all coming together." Emmie said.

Sam and Emmie continue to ride through the open pasture with the sun starting to dip behind the mountains. The herd of horses make a path and keep their distance.

* * *

The next morning finds Sam, cup of coffee in hand, exiting the house and walking on the porch.

"Honey?" The silence has Sam a little worried. But his nerves are put to rest when he hears Emmie's voice down at round pen. Stepping down from the porch, Sam takes a sip of coffee, and heads towards the holding pens.

Sam leans his arms and head just over the rail of the round pen and peers into the small arena. In the early light of dawn is a sight that brings a smile to his face. Emmie, her faded brown cowboy hat on and pants tucked into her boots, stands in the middle of the round pen. Making laps around her is her sorrel mare, Reba. At Reba's side is a three month old paint colt.

Sam steps up and rests his arms on the top rail of the round pen.

"You sure got up early this morning," Sam said.

"Sam Murray, of all people, you should know this ain't early," Emmie says, her whole face smiling over at him.

"Yeah, yeah," Sam replies.

"Just us new moms getting some exercise," Emmie said.

Sam sets his coffee mug on the ground and crawls through the wooden fence. He walks to the center to join Emmie.

"How is ol' Reba this morning?" Sam said with a whistle. At the sound of the command, Reba stops, turns, and walks up to him. Sam gives her a big pet on the neck. "What a good mare this is."

"This colt is gonna be a good horse for our children." Emmie said watching the paint colt trot to Reba's side. "What are we going to do with all these babies running around?"

"Raise the biggest family you've ever seen." Sam said with a smile.

Emmie nods her head in agreement. Her joy is cut short by a sharp pain she feels deep in her belly. She holds her stomach to steady herself, sucking her breath, and then quickly doubles over because the pain comes harder.

She groans, eyes closed hard, teeth clenched tight. Sam is instantly at her side.

"Honey, are you alright?" Sam said trying to hide the worry in his voice.

Emmie, in obvious pain, raises her head and gasps the words, "I think it's time."

"Alright, we've got this."

Sam runs hard for the Ford pickup truck, returning as fast as he can and stopping next to the round pen. Jumping out and leaving the driver side door open, he goes to Emmie's side. Helping her away from the fence, he opens the passenger door and gently sets her inside.

"Hang in there honey, it won't be long now," Sam said, doing his best to stay positive. He reaches over to touch her shoulder, wincing as she curls over on the bench seat in pain, moaning as though she's being pulled apart.

The Murray's pickup flies down the dirt road away from the ranch. With storm clouds forming on the horizon the pickup truck drives under the wooden arch that reads *Murray Ranch*, turning onto the main highway.

Chapter 4

Sam made record time on the forty five

mile trip to Sheridan. Halfway there, the

storm clouds fully formed and burst, dumping a

fierce and pelting rain onto the windshield of

the pickup. Not an unusual occurrence for the

middle of July but it did test Sam's driving

ability, keeping one eye on the road while the

other helplessly watched Emmie. Only twenty

eight, Sam had been through some of life's

ordeals but hearing Emmie's cries of pain and

not being able to do anything ranked at the top.

By the time the truck made its way down the main street of Sheridan, the heavy rains had faded to a drizzle, bouncing off the windshield as the pickup truck turns left and the Sheridan Hospital comes into view. Sam screeches to a stop in front of the emergency entrance.

Jumping from the truck, Sam yelled, "We need some help!" to two nurses standing at the door of the hospital. "The baby - - it's not time!"

Armed with a wheelchair, the nurses made their way quickly while Sam gently helped Emmie from the truck and into the chair. They began wheeling Emmie into the hospital, Sam close behind.

"Sir, please, we will handle it from here," the nurse said, stopping Sam at the door.

Again, the helpless feeling comes as he watches his wife being wheeled into the hospital.

"I love you!" He yelled as the hospital doors close behind the wheelchair, but the only sound Sam can hear is the rain bouncing off his hat.

* * *

If it had been five minutes, one hour, or a full day, Sam could not tell you. He paced, he sat, he was nervous with questions no one seemed able to answer. The nurse at the reception desk was starting to feel Sam's pain every time he looked her way and her only answer to his nervous query was a regretful shake of her head.

The small waiting room did have others in it, but everyone was wrapped in their own worries and so it remained quiet. Sam finally sat with his head in his hands, doing the only thing he could: wait.

"Mr. Murray…?" the doctor said entering the waiting room and looking about.

At the sound of his name, Sam jumps out of his chair. "What's going on?" Sam demanded. "Why is it taking so long?"

With his hand on Sam's shoulder, he said, "Mr. Murray, please come with me."

"What is going on?" Sam said not moving.

Exhaling, the doctor met Sam's eyes and said, "There were complications during the delivery."

"Complications?" Sam asks. "What kind of complications?"

"Your son is in perfect health," the doctor answered, holding his hand up in a stopping motion, trying to assure Sam and keep him calm.

The words hit Sam like a truck. His son. His son is healthy; his son.

"I have a son?" Sam replies.

The doctor nods his head, a tight smile on his lips, and then gestures towards the door again. "Please, come with me," he said.

Sam follows the doctor out of the waiting room and towards the delivery rooms. As they exit, he notices Lester Morgan, once one of the best ranchers and biggest land-owners in the county, enter the waiting room. Lester, not seeing Sam or any other familiar face, takes a seat and starts waiting like all the others in the room.

Emmie is cradling their new born, Kade, on her chest as Sam and the doctor enter the delivery room. She looks weak, tired, and visibly in pain, but the edges of her mouth lift in a slight smile as he approaches and says, "you were right. We have a son." Sam moves quickly to her side, taking in her pale skin, her lips barely visible.

He touches her cheek gently and says, "Honey, you did it. He's perfect."

Emmie tries to speak but can't muster any words. She exhales, whispering, "I'm so tired. I just need to close my eyes for a minute." She lifts her eyes away from her son, turning from the baby to look into Sam's worried eyes, her own eyes already half closed.

"God, he is beautiful, he looks just like you," Sam said.

With a slight nod in agreement, Emmie finds the strength to hand the baby to his father. Sam gently takes Kade from his mother and looks into his eyes. Sam, tearing up, looks at Emmie who is closing her eyes.

Sam stands, handing the baby to a nurse.

"Honey...?" Sam says gently cupping Emmie's face.

Her eyes flutter open and she whispers, "He's so lucky. Two great men to learn from."

"What complications are you talking about?" Sam asks the doctor over his shoulder.

"There is massive internal bleeding. We can't stop it. I'm sorry, Mr. Murray, but you should say your goodbyes while there's time."

"No. No!" Sam says, turning back to face Emmie, whose eyes have closed again, in the bed. He scoops her shoulders with his arm, burying his head in her neck. "I need you. Honey, don't you leave me. I need you. I can't do this by myself," he cries into the strands of her brown hair. "Honey, you stay with us!" He feels her hands move lightly to his waist and her voice in his ear, "I love you, Sam Murray," before her hands drop away.

Suddenly, the hospital equipment starts beeping. Sam's heart rate jumps, matching the beeping of the equipment. The doctor has moved rapidly to Emmie's side, pushing Sam to the side.

"What's that mean?" Sam asks, now standing back and rubbing his sweaty palms on his jeans.

"Mr. Murray, please stay back," the doctor said, holding his hand out and stopping him from approaching again.

"What is going on?" Sam demanded.

"Mr. Murray, let us work," the doctor said, turning back to Emmie.

In the waiting room, Lester and the other patrons hear a commotion as several staff rush through.

The heart rate monitor goes flat. Sam ignores the doctor and rushes to Emmie's side. He grabs her hand squeezes tight, yet his hand is not being gripped back. Tears stream down his face as his mouth is open but no words come out. The doctor puts his arm around Sam but he pushes it away. He won't let go of Emmie's hand.

"Mr. Murray…" The nurse said. "Mr. Murray…"

Sam just stares into Emmie's still face.

"Mr. Murray…"

* * *

Sam leans up against the hospital nursery glass staring at his son. He is numb, no expression visible on his face. He doesn't seem to notice the nurse approach with a nursery bag.

"Mr. Murray, we are so sorry for your loss," the nurse said, waiting for a response. "The other nurses and I put together this bag for you to help with your son. There are some bottles and cloth diapers."

Sam just stares at baby Kade.

"Well...I'll just leave this bag right here for you," The nurse said.

Sam gives a slight nod and puts his hand on the glass, watching his son sleep.

Chapter 5

Sam's Ford pickup truck turns off the main highway and drives under the *Murray Ranch* arch. The tires kick up drying mud as the vehicle makes its way to the ranch house. The horses in the closest pasture notice the truck and run alongside the fence line as it passes.

Sam pulls into the ranch yard and parks. The setting sun sends a glare through the windshield. Averting his eyes, Sam looks at baby Kade, still sound asleep, next to him. Exhaling and looking at the ranch through the windshield, the weight of the task ahead seems to push down on his shoulders. Sam slouches forward with his forehead resting on the steering wheel.

After another deep breath, Sam exits the truck and closes the door gently, so as not to wake Kade. What's ahead, what's been lost, and what's been gained, crashes on his shoulders. Sam falls to his knees.

"God damn it!" Sam yells.

Steadying himself with the pickup truck, Sam gets back to his feet. The outburst seems to have relieved a touch of stress and pain, at least enough to allow him to collect his thoughts. It also, happily, did not wake Kade. Staring at him through the driver's window, Sam almost envied him, sleeping soundly without a care in the world. Almost, because Sam can't escape the thought that the baby is the reason his beloved Emmie is gone.

After entering the house, Sam sets the still sleeping Kade on the couch. Tossing the nursery bag on the ground, he enters the kitchen, opens a cabinet, pulling out a bottle of whiskey. Finding a glass, Sam pours himself a drink and knocks it back as he stares out the window. His gaze is fixed on the horses down in the holding pens. Just another job that needs to be done. He looks in the empty glass, pondering an ever growing list of tasks and pours another drink.

He begins to lift the glass when Kade's cry interrupts him. Turning slowly, Sam is surprised at the feeling of anger he has towards the baby. He downs his drink and goes over to him. Picking up the crying bundle, Sam starts to walk around the living room. He tries to soothe Kade's crying but nothing seems to work. His anger seems to rise until he looks into Kade's eyes.

"You have your mama's eyes," Sam said in surprise.

Kade continues wailing.

"Are you hungry? Is that it?" Sam said glancing at the nursery bag.

Pulling a premade bottle out of the bag, Sam puts it to Kade's lips. Kade quickly latches on and begins to drink. With the crying stopped and his son nursing, calmness comes over Sam.

"That-a boy." Sam says proudly.

***

A week has passed since Sam brought Kade home. There have been some rough spells and learning curves, but Sam has managed. He hasn't had much time to think, which in a way has been the most beneficial. If you are at the bottom of a well, sometimes it's best not to look up.

Sam stands holding Kade as dusk arrives on the land. They are underneath a large tree that overlooks a breathtaking valley, his favorite spot on the ranch. Sam does his best to smile and speak but his emotions are getting the best of him. At his feet is the grave of Emmie.

"Well, sweetheart, here's Kade," Sam says, tearing up and biting his hand in clenched teeth. He gathers himself with a couple choking breaths, and then adjusts Kade as he kneels down. "God, I miss you, honey. How can I raise this boy without you?"

Sam's heartfelt emission is interrupted by Kade, who starts to cry.

"Hungry again?" Sam said. He places a flower on Emmie's grave before he stands up. "I love you, sweetheart."

Wiping tears from his eyes, Sam turns and walks away from the large tree, carrying Kade.

Across the property line, yet still in view, stands Lester. His Rafter M Morgan Ranch is the closest neighbor to the Murrays. He is far enough away that he cannot be seen but he can see. Stroking his beard, he shakes his head in disappointment and turns away.

Sam, holding Kade, enters the ranch house from the kitchen door. He is comforting Kade as he digs in the nursery bag for a bottle. The bag is empty. Searching the kitchen, Sam can't find anything close to a bottle or even milk. Knowing Kade will become more upset, he sets him down so he can perform a double handed search through the kitchen.

Still nothing can be found. Sam comes across his bottle of whiskey. He looks at the bottle in his hand. His first reaction is to take a pull but the crying Kade demands his attention. Sam sets the bottle of whiskey on the kitchen counter. In doing so, he spots a small herd of cows through the kitchen window. An idea starts to form as he turns to Kade.

"Well, it's about time you learned how things work around here," Sam said.

Picking up Kade, Sam opens the kitchen door. With his free hand, he grabs a pair of leather work gloves on a shelf and stuffs them in his pocket.

***

Sam rides his horse across a pasture of the ranch. Kade is strapped to him in a papoose, given to Emmie by a friend who lives north on the reservation. The sun has set but there is still enough light for Sam to spot the same small herd of cows. Riding next to a tree, he pulls rein and steps off. Taking the papoose off, he sets it, with Kade, next to the tree.

"It's all right son, Dad will be right back," Sam said with determination.

Stepping back up on his horse, Sam pulls his rope out. He turns his horse towards the herd and lopes off in their direction. He slows to a walk as he approaches so he won't spook the cows. Stopping, he picks out the fattest cow with the largest milk bag.

Back at the tree, Kade has started whining. Riding on the horse had soothed his hunger away for a time, but now it's back. Curious of the noise, Reba's paint colt has come to the tree to investigate. Spotting Kade, the colt approaches him cautiously. Once close enough, the colt stretches his nose to smell. With the colt's muzzle close enough to blow hot air on Kade's face, he stops crying.

Sam has cut the large cow away from the small herd. He is in chase, swinging his rope. With his focus concentrated on the task at hand he does not notice the bovine changes direction and is headed right for Kade. The cow is just far enough ahead of Sam he can't throw his rope yet.

Sam, now seeing the path the cow is on, does not have the time or speed to stop her. His eyes get large as the bovine gets closer to Kade. Suddenly, the paint colt pins his ears back and gets between the cow and Kade. The cow turns back right into Sam's range and he ropes it. He puts a dally on his saddle horn followed by a quick half hitch.

With the chase over and the cow tight on the end of the rope, Sam dismounts his horse.

"Thanks, pard," Sam says, looking back at the paint colt.

Using the rope as an extension of his hand, Sam eases his way towards the cow. The bovine jumps around a bit but settles as Sam gets closer. Pulling the gloves from his pocket, He slowly kneels down and begins to milk the cow. The leather gloves are catching the milk.

Petting the cow, Sam stands back up and carries the milk filled gloves back to the tree. The paint colt has started to graze about ten feet away. Kneeling down, Sam uses his pocket knife to poke a hole in the index finger of the glove. Kade quickly latches on and starts to drink.

"There, you go. See? Your old man can take care of you." Sam said almost reassuring himself.

Sam, leading the milk cow, rides back to the barn in the dark, a sleeping and content Kade strapped to him. Two horse lengths behind the roped cow is the paint colt. Sam turns back to admire the small cavalcade, and the colt in the rear.

"Son, it looks like you made your first friend," Sam said smiling.

Chapter 6

A few days have gone by and Sam enters the kitchen carrying some new baby bottles. After setting them on the kitchen counter, he walks over and picks up Kade. Kade is smiling and showing off his big hazel eyes. A schedule has now formed and Sam knows a supper time feeding is minutes away. Grabbing one of the bottles, he fills it with fresh cow's milk.

He puts the the lid on the bottle, and his gaze wanders towards the Morgan ranch. Through the kitchen window, the distant view shows the vague outlines of buildings on the horizon. With the bottle ready he lets Kade latch on and start to drink. Sam's eyes continue to stare as his mind drifts.

***

A week ago was Emmie's funeral. The pastor from the county church performed the service under the large tree. The parishioners from the church were there as well. They filled the area with words of love and songs of faith. Sam stands by the open gravesite alone. In the back, behind everyone, stood Lester.

Even as Sam remembers the service now, it's a blur. It started, then friends spoke about Emmie, giving words of encouragement and condolences. He shook hands and hugged neighbors, and then one by one, they were gone. He was offered help to bury the casket but that's something Sam wanted to do alone.

The deed nearly done, Sam shoveled the last few scoops of dirt on the grave. Having watched from afar, Lester approached as Sam stood up and leaned against his shovel.

"It was a nice service," Lester said. "Thank you for that."

Sam, paying Lester no mind, began to shovel again.

"Can I give you a hand with that?" Lester asks.

"I got it," Sam replies without looking at him.

Lester looks back towards his ranch and said, "You know, there is a pretty spot over on my place that you could have used. It would have been perfect."

Sam stops shoveling and looks at Lester.

"She belongs here," Sam said.

"Where's the baby? Shouldn't he have been here for this?" Lester asks.

"He's had his supper and he's sleeping at the house. I didn't want him around all this." Sam said.

A distant cry can be heard from the ranch house.

"You got no idea what you're doing," Lester said shaking his head.

"What's that supposed to mean?" Sam asked, his temper staring to rise.

"I think you know exactly what it means," Lester retorts. "You're just like your old man. Everyone knows he drank himself to death."

"You better watch your mouth, you ain't no angel yourself." Sam said, pointing his finger at Lester. "I think it's time for you to go home."

"Don't think you can brush me off, Sam." Lester replies, his blood starting to boil.

"Save your breath, Les, I have to go. I want you off my property!" Sam said making a point.

"Your property, huh?" Lester said, looking Sam right in the eye. "That's how it's gonna be?"

Sam returns Lester's angry stare with his own. "That's how it's gonna be," Sam replies.

Lester sets his jaw, turning on his heel and walking away. Sam sticks the spade shovel in the ground next to Emmie's grave. Watching Lester walk away, Sam's temper begins to recede. He takes a deep breath then walks back towards the ranch house to check on Kade.

* * *

So much has happened since Emmie's service he hasn't had any time to reflect on the matter. Sam starts to get upset, mostly at himself, because it's the memory of his neighbor that helped him do so. He doesn't want any help from Lester, even when it comes to thinking.

Kade, having finished his bottle, has fallen asleep in Sam's arms. He walks him over to the make-shift crib he has put together. The real crib is in the shop; he thought he had another month to finish it. In the mean time some large pillows and a couch cushion work. Sam lays his sleeping baby down.

Knowing Kade is full and sleeping soundly; Sam goes into the kitchen and pulls out his bottle of whiskey. He pours himself a drink but stops. Again, he finds himself looking out the kitchen window towards his neighbor's ranch. Pondering for a moment, he looks at the whiskey bottle, and then glances towards Kade. He nods his head, and without hesitation, pours the bottle of whiskey down the kitchen sink.

To clear his head, Sam walks outside to get a breath of fresh air. Hands in his jacket pocket, he walks down to the holding pens and leans on the corral. Looking up at the stars, he does not notice the paint colt walk over to him until the warm breath blows on his wrist. Sam smiles and scratches the colt's neck.

"Well, if it isn't my little helper, Pard," Sam said, continuing to pet the young horse. "So you seem to like Kade." Sam pause a moment then nods his head. "Yeah, me too."

Chapter 7

1954.

    Sam trots his horse through a green pasture, stopping his horse next to a barbed wire gate. Dismounting, Sam uses his shoulder to release pressure on the gate post. Opening the gate, Sam leads his horse through the slot. He looks at the empty hills behind him and listens. He hears the faint sounds he is straining for and remounts his horse, moving away from the gate.

Over the green hills crest a small herd of horned cattle. They are mostly in a line, spread three across. The herd moved at a good pace because, behind them, keeping them moving is Kade. Eight years old now, Kade wears his own weather beaten felt cowboy hat. His brown chaps make noise as he bounces his rope off of them. The sound helped keep the cattle moving.

Kade's mount is the paint colt, grown now, into a beautiful horse. The colt was trained and affectionately named Pard, by Sam. Kade and Pard work as a team pushing the cattle towards the open gate.

"Don't let them get around you, son!" Sam called, watching the cattle slow down and try to scatter near the gate opening.

Without hesitation, Kade pushes Pard closer to the herd. They get them back in line and push the cattle through the barbed wire gate.

"Keep pushing the cows and I'll meet you back at the corrals," Sam said, as Kade rides through the gate.

Kade gave a head nod, not unlike his father's, as he and Pard continue to drive the cattle towards the barn and holding pens. Sam walked his horse to the gate, sliding off to close it. As he grabbed the saddle horn to re-mount, Sam proudly smiled over his horse, watching his young son doing a man's job.

Approaching the holding pens, Sam pulls up next to the corral gate. Kade, on foot, is already dropping the latch.

"Good job, cowboy." Sam said.

"Thank you, sir," Kade said, crawling back onto Pard.

"How many did you count?" Sam asked.

"Twenty-three." Kade said.

"Alright, now if you add these cows to the rest of the herd in the east pasture, how many do we have?" Sam said.

"I forgot how many are in the east pasture." Kade asked.

"Fifty-six," Sam replied.

Kade, thinking hard, picturing all his fingers and toes. "Seventy…nine?"

"Are you sure?" Sam asked.

"Yes," Kade said feeling sure of himself.

"Nice job," Sam said with a reassuring head nod. "Now, don't forget that number."

"Yes, sir," Kade replied, admiring the cattle in the corral.

"Well, come on, the works over here," Sam said, turning his horse towards the barn. Kade wheeled Pard around and rode up to his father's side.

Sam's unsaddled horse stands tied to the hitch'n rail inside the barn. Kade is trying

54

to unsaddle Pard, also tied to the rail. Frustration is setting in because Pard is just a little tall for the eight year old.

"Down, Pard," Kade said, clucking to the horse. Pard does nothing. "Down Pard!" Again, Pard does nothing. "Dad, I can't get Pard to kneel," Kade said, feeling defeated.

"Kade, don't lose your patience," Sam said, exiting the tack room, next to the hitch'n rail. "The minute that happens, you lose control of the situation. He doesn't know it, you gotta teach him. Remember what I told you," Sam makes a downward motion with his hand. "Use your hand."

"Down, Pard," this time mimicking his father's hand motion.

Pard, at the sight and sound of the command, kneels down on his front legs. The height difference is erased and Kade begins to loosen the cinch on his saddle.

Feeling proud of the well trained Pard, "There, you see." Sam said.

"Thanks, Dad." Kade replied carrying his saddle into the tack room.

***

Sam, sitting with his saddle between his legs, finished fixing some cracked leather latigos. The setting sun could be seen through the open barn doors. After admiring his work, Sam stood up and carried his saddle back into the tack room.

In the breezeway of the barn, Kade was playing with his rope. He was trying his best to perform a rope trick called "the butterfly." The vertical loop of a roper dances around them at a high rate of speed, hard to master even for the most talented ropers. Kade tries as he might but was unsuccessful.

Sam exits the tack room carrying Kade's saddle, "Son, the works over here."

"But Dad, I think I almost got it," Kade replied optimistically.

"You mean, 'have it.'"

"Yes sir, have it. I almost have it," Kade corrected himself.

"You practice every day, there will be plenty more time later," Sam said, setting Kade's saddle on the ground. "Right now I want to look your saddle over. Make sure the stirrup leathers aren't ripped or cracked." Kade set his rope down and joined his father. "We always want our tack in the best shape. No accidents for next Saturday."

"When we help out the Petersons?" Kade said.

"Yep," Sam replied.

Father and son start to look Kade's saddle over with a fine tooth comb. The sound of a tractor trailer's airbrakes penetrate the barn. Curiously, Sam looks in that direction. He sets the saddle down and motions to Kade to follow him. Kade, a thin kid, hikes his jeans up as he accompanies his dad out of the barn.

Chapter 8

A nineteen fifties red Peterbilt stock
truck and trailer had stopped at the Murray
Ranch gate. The passenger side door opens and
a set of new cowboy boots step down from the
running boards. George Goodman scanned the
horizon and read the ranch sign.

"Thank you much," George says, shutting
the Peterbilt's door. Planting his boots, a
size too big, on the ground, he tips his clean
straw cowboy hat back on his head. Glancing up

the dirt driveway, George can see the setting
sun falling behind the ranch buildings.

Exiting the barn, Sam and Kade looked
down the dirt road to see the commotion. The
Peterbilt could be heard going into gear and
driving away, leaving the tall man standing at
the ranch entrance.

"Dad, who is that?" Kade asked.

Sam replied, shaking his head, "I don't
know, son." Sam put his arm around Kade and
urged him forward as they walked down the dirt
driveway to greet the newcomer.

George, a man in his early thirties, gave
the truck one last wave before putting his
straw hat back on his head. Picking up his
duffel bag, he began to walk into the Murray
Ranch. His newly bought silver spurs jingling
as he walked. Shading his eyes from the
setting sun, he walked to meet the two people
proceeding to greet him.

"Can I help you?" Sam said when he and Kade were within speaking distance.

"No sir, I believe I can help you," George said with all the confidence in the world.

Skeptical, Sam took a protective step in front of Kade. "How do you figure that, stranger?"

"The name is George. George Goodman…cowboy for hire," George replied, almost trying to convince himself.

"Well, George, I think you have the wrong…" Sam said before he was interrupted.

"No sir, everyone in town said Sam Murray needs help," George interjected. "Here I am."

Sam measured George for a cool second, his eyes landed on the bright silver spurs he wore. "Is that so. What exactly can you help with?" Sam asked.

"Back in town they said it's just you and your boy running this ranch. You need all the help you can get." George said.

"I appreciate the concern, friend, but Kade and I…" Sam said again being interrupted.

"Need my help." George again interjected.

"Determined feller aren't you?" Sam said, shaking his head. The confidence of this stranger was starting to make Sam think he should hear him out. "Where have you worked George?"

"The Five Star…" George said then paused.

"The Five Star Ranch, down by Laramie?" Sam asked, clearly surprised.

George was shaking his head. "The Five Star Deli…Trenton, New Jersey?" He said it like a question, hoping it wasn't a deal breaker. "I make the best damn pastrami sandwich on the East Coast." George noticed

Kade look sharply at Sam. "Excuse my language."

"What do you know about ranching?" Sam asked completely dumbfounded.

"I know my meats and cheeses," George replied with the last bit of confidence he could muster.

"Is this some type of joke?" Sam quickly replied.

Taking a deep breath, having put all his chips on the table, George looked Sam in the eye. "No sir, I came out west to be a cowboy. Just like in all those books I've read," he said sincerely.

"Books, huh?" Sam said as if he just read the revealing chapter of George's story. "Is that why you look like you walked out of the *Sears Catalog*?"

Kade watched George look his clothes over. His jeans were too short, his yellow checked shirt too stiff, his straw hat perfectly clean and un-scuffed boots. He looked like a kid playing dress up cowboy. George knew his appearance and lack of experience weren't being received well.

"Give me a chance, Mr. Murray," George pleaded.

Sam, not showing it, admired the confidence George had. To leave what you know and head west on a dream; stories like that are from a hundred years ago. For almost a decade, Sam had been concentrating on two things: raising Kade and working this ranch. He almost forgot there was an East Coast until George mentioned it. An extra set of hands would help, and at the very least George would have the strength of a man, not an eight year old boy.

Sam looked at Kade, "What do you think, Kade?" as he was staring at George. "Should we give this tinhorn a chance?" Kade turned and gave an enthusiastic head nod. "Alright George, the boss agrees. We'll give you a try." Kade smiled at what his father said. "Ten bucks a month, a good horse to ride and all the beans you can eat."

George's face lit up as his eyes got as large as silver dollars. "I get to ride a horse?" he asked, clearly unable to contain his joy any longer. "Thank you…thank you, Mr. Murray," he looked at Kade as well. "You won't regret this."

Sam shook George's hand to seal the deal. "We'll see." Sam pointed to the ranch barn. "We've got a bunk in the barn, follow us." Sam and Kade turned and began to walk towards the ranch buildings. George threw his duffel bag on his shoulder and quickly followed behind them.

Entering the barn, George noticed Pard tied to the hitch'n rail. He set his duffel bag down and approached the horse, petting his neck gently.

Sam gestures toward a horse stall in the back of the barn. "The bunk is back there, George. It ain't much but it beats sleeping on the ground."

"That will be fine, thank you again." George said, continuing to pet Pard.

Kade had noticed George's interest in his horse. "His name is Pard; he's mine," Kade explained.

"What a beautiful steed," George replied. "I hope to have one of my own someday." Stroking the horse, George's confidence started to return. "Animals love me."

To punctuate George's statement, Pard swished his tail, whipping the ends across George's face. The move caught George by surprise, stinging his eyes. Wincing, he stumbled backwards, tripping over his spurs. Kade covered his mouth to keep a laugh from escaping. Not finding the incident funny, Sam shakes his head.

"Kade, why don't you put Pard away," Sam said. "I'll meet you back at the house."

"Yes, sir." Kade replied, collecting his composure. He untied Pard and led the horse by George, out of the barn.

Sam turns his attention to George. "Why don't you get settled in and we'll see you in the morning." Sam started to walk away but stopped, looking back at George. "By the way…you earn spurs around here, you don't just buy them." Sam, not waiting for a response, turned on his heel and left the barn.

George was never good at first impressions, but this one took the cake. He watched Sam leave, stuck there in a situation of his own making.

Chapter 9

Sam and Kade stood on the front porch embracing a new day. The sun had not yet risen and darkness still engulfed the ranch yard. Sam, as usual for this time of day, sipped his cup of coffee. Kade was located at his father's side, yawning. Meeting the day before the sun rose was nothing new for these two but this morning had a tinge of excitement about it.

Their anticipation was answered when George, wearing the same clothes from yesterday, emerged from the barn.

"Morning George. How did the barn treat you?" Sam asked.

"Fine…just fine," George replied, rubbing his back.

"Glad to hear it. Grab a cup of coffee and let's get to work," Sam said. Turning to Kade, "Son, fetch the horses." Pausing as if to solve a puzzle, Sam continued, "Grab Reba for George."

"Yes, sir." Kade answered with a stretch and yawn.

"George and I will meet you at the tack room."

Kade nodded his head and walked off the porch, passing George on his way.

"Good morning, Mr. Goodman," Kade said.

"Good morning, kid," George replied.

In the barn, Kade tied the three horses to the hitch'n rail. Sam and George entered, sipping their steaming coffee. Kade emerges from the tack room carrying the grooming bucket and was ready to start.

Handing a brush to George, Kade said, "You're going to be riding my mother's horse, Reba."

"Well, okay," George replied. He wanted so badly to fit in and Kade seemed to have no prejudice towards him, so he continued, "Where is your mother?"

The question caught Kade off guard, which could be seen on his face. Kade looked to his dad for guidance.

"Go ahead," Sam said, nodding his head with encouragement.

"She passed when I was born," Kade said clearing a lump in his throat. Pausing a second, Kade points at Reba, "And that's her horse you'll be riding." Kade's eyes drift down to George's silver spurs. "You might want to take your spurs off."

"I'll be alright, kid," George said trying to save face.

"Your call, Mr. Goodman," Kade replied with a laugh.

Sam, watched this exchange, interjected, "The work's over here, grab a brush and get her cleaned up."

"Here you go," Kade said, handing George a brush. Turning away, Kade starts grooming Pard, the scratch of the brushes the only sound in the morning air.

George walked over to Reba, looking at the brush. Watching Kade and Sam perform the job on their horses, George starts on Reba. The mare always enjoyed the brush so she stood still.

"There you go, girl," George said smiling. He looked Sam's direction and continued, "I think I can get the hang of this." A fly settled on one of Reba's front legs, prompting her to stomp it. In doing so, she landed on George's foot, and then continued to stand still as she had before the fly. "Ahhhh!" He yelled, "Help me!"

Sam and Kade turned from their grooming to see what had happened. Kade immediately went to Reba's shoulder and lightly touched her, moving her off George's foot. Sam shakes his head in disappointment as George hopped around on one foot.

"George, why don't you go in the tack room and grab the first saddle on the right hand side," Sam explained.

"Yeah…Yeah sure," George said as he began to put weight on his flattened foot. As he limped to the tack room, Sam looked at Kade and raised his eyebrows. Kade responded with a shoulder shrug.

George's attention was still on his foot when he entered the tack room doorway and did not notice the low door jam. He smashed his noggin into the header of the tack room, crunching a crease in his new straw hat. "Ouch!" he yelled.

Once again, Sam and Kade turned to look in George's direction.

"Come on George, the work's over here," Sam said losing his patience with this so called cowboy for hire. Kade stopped a giggle before it started, as he knew by looking at his father, now is not the time.

***

The morning dawned bright and clear, as Sam, Kade, and George sat their horses overlooking a small herd of cows.

"Now, let's go nice and slow and move this herd to the north pasture," Sam said pointing the way with his index finger. "Kade, you head down there and get the cows moving in the right direction. George, you follow Kade." Sam paused and looked right at George, "Try and stay out of trouble." He turned to Kade and continued, "I'll open the gates."

"Alright kid, lead the way." George said as he looked at Kade. Kade nodded his head in agreement and began to ride towards the herd. George gave Reba a kick with his spurs as Kade began to ride past. Reba, having felt the cue, jumped forward as asked, dumping George on the ground.

The sound of the commotion turned Kade's head. Seeing George on the ground, Kade trotted Pard back to George. "You all right?" he asked.

George rubbed his backside, as he slowly got up. Reba had not moved, and was looking at him. "Yeah…Yeah I'm ok." He said grabbing Reba's reins. George could feel Sam's eyes on him.

"Come on George, even the horse knows you ain't qualified to wear those spurs," Sam explained. "Kade told you that."

George never looked at Sam as he knelt down and unstrapped his spurs. He stood up and hung them from his saddle horn. "They never fit right anyways," George said, convincing himself it was his own idea.

Sam turned his horse towards the gate and yelled back, "Come on boys, the work's over here."

Kade, still next to George, said "You're gonna hear that a lot, Mr. Goodman."

George collected his composure and crawled back on Reba. He let her pick her own pace as they followed Kade to the herd of cows.

From his position, near the open gate, Sam watched as Kade and to some effect, George, gathered the cows. In his eyes, Kade still had so much to learn, but being paired with George made him look like the greatest cowboy on the northern plains. Kade did ninety-five percent of the work as George flopped and hung onto Reba for dear life. If Reba wasn't such a seasoned ranch horse, the small roundup could have been much worse.

Kade and George pushed the cows towards the open gate. A few heifers tried to turn back and run but Kade and Pard put a quick stop to it. As the critters made their way through the gate, Kade pulled rein and George did the same.

"Not bad," Sam said as he pulled the barbed wire gate shut. "Not bad at all."

Kade always liked hearing an acknowledgement of a job well done from his father. George was surprised how it made him feel; maybe he could do this. As Sam stepped back up on his horse, the faint sound of a calf crying could be heard. The trio turned their heads in that direction.

Kade rode Pard to the edge of a hill in the direction the noise was coming from. Turning back towards Sam and George, he yelled "Dad, I think there's a calf stuck in the mud!" Upon hearing this Sam, with George following, joined Kade. Down the hill about twenty-five feet, a newborn calf was lying down with its hind legs buried in a mud hole. The young bovine was trying to crawl forward, balling, to no avail.

"Let's ease on down…" Sam said, but paused, because George had already dismounted and was making his way towards the trapped animal.

Tip toeing through the mud, George got behind the scared calf. Not being able to move made it easy for George to start to push the young calf out of the mud hole.

Sam watched, semi-impressed with George's eagerness to help, but again, he showed a lack of judgment. "George, take it easy," Sam said.

"Here you go, buddy," George said, solely concentrated on helping the calf. From the treeline, its mama arrived on a dead run, responding to her baby's bawling, trampling George into the mud. With the commotion, the calf broke free and lunged forward out of the mud pit.

Kade's eyes are wide from the scene he witnessed. Sam sat with no expression on his face, thinking, 'can someone really have that poor of luck?' Kade pulled his rope out and threw it out to George. He grabbed the rope as Kade dallied up and pulled him out.

Kade coiled his rope back up as George, his front covered in mud, sat at the edge of the bog.

"Come on boys, the work's over here," Sam said, shaking his head and turning his horse toward the open pasture.

***

Sam and Kade are clearing the dinner table, having just finished eating supper.

"Dad, do you think Mr. Goodman is gonna be alright?" Kade asked as he carried his dirty plate to the kitchen.

"After the day he had, I can see why he just wanted to lie down and skip supper," Sam answered. With the ketchup in one hand, he opened up the refrigerator door. "We're about out of food. We better make a trip into town tomorrow," Sam said, examining the contents of the fridge. "Have you finished that book yet?" Sam asked, as he closed the refrigerator and looked at Kade.

"I finished it last night before bed," Kade responded.

"Good." We'll get you another one tomorrow as well," Sam said. Running the day's events back through his mind, Sam asked, "Son, do you like this cowboy life?"

"Yeah, of course," Kade said, turning to face his father. "Especially because I'm so much better at it than you," Kade laughed.

Sam smiled, "You are definitely better at it than someone we know." Kade laughed again as Sam continued, "Besides, you have a great teacher."

With the moon starting to rise through the house windows, Sam enters Kade's bedroom. Kade, already in bed, turns towards his dad, as he tucks him in.

"Did you say your prayers?" Sam asked.

"Yes, sir," Kade replied.

"Good job today, cowboy," Sam said as he tucked Kade in. "Get a good night's rest. We're gonna visit your mom tomorrow." Sam stood back up and began to walk out of the room.

"Love you, Dad," Kade said.

Turning, Sam replied, "I love you too, kiddo." Switching the light off, Sam walked out of the room.

Chapter 10

George was standing behind the barn, wearing nothing but his boxer shorts and boots, answering nature's call. It was a brisk morning but the cool air was waking him up. He could not remember the last time he slept so hard, his bunk could have been a ladder and wouldn't have made a difference. It was his hope he was the first one up, to show he was ready, that he still had some try left in him.

That idea was dashed when he heard Kade's voice from the other side of the barn, "Can I drive, Dad?" He finished his business, and thought, 'what time do cowboys get up?' George rounded the barn and saw Sam and Kade standing next to the pickup.

"We'll see. Maybe on the way back," Sam said, opening the passenger side door for Kade. As Kade hopped in, Sam spotted George. "Morning, George." Shutting the door, Sam walked to the driver's side, taking in George's attire. He was not the least bit surprised by the way George was dressed. "What do you think of this cowboying?" he asked.

"I've learned one thing about cowboying: the work is always over there," George replied.

With a laugh, Sam said, "Despite everything you have done, I'm glad you're here today." George creased his brow at the statement as Sam continued. "Kade and I need to head into town. The horse shoer is coming out this afternoon. If we're not back in time, you help him out. He knows which horses to start on."

"Ok, sure," George said.

"Help yourself to some coffee at the house. There's also a couple strips of bacon left. If you want more, you'll get up earlier," Sam said with a smile.

Reluctantly nodding his head in agreement, George said, "Thank you." As Sam got into the pickup, George asked, "How will I know who the horse shoer is?"

"Oh, you'll know," Sam said shutting the door, with the window down he continued, "His name is Red. Red Burk."

The Ford started up and George watched it drive away from the barn. He took a deep breath and clapped his hands. He smiled as he thought to himself, 'the work's over here.'

***

The Sheridan City Café was located in the middle of town, across Main Street from Howard's General Store. The diagonal parking spaces in front of the café were always full during the breakfast hour. Along with the best specials in town, the café also offered a beautiful view of the growing main street.

Sitting at the table closest to the windows was Lester. He was joined by three other elder town statesmen: Walter Sims, Harv Northcott, and Ben Brown. Younger men would congregate at the saloon, but being in their sixties, these men bust each other's chops over coffee and eggs. Yet if you asked them, they tell you they were solving the world's problems.

"So, like I was saying, those heifers fell through the fence and ended up on the main highway," said Harv. His hat was sitting on the table revealing his white hair that matched his perfectly groomed mustache. "If it wasn't for the Sheriff driving by at the right time, I would have lost twenty to thirty head."

"If you ever checked your fence Harv, you'd have a healthy bottom line," Ben said as he pulled a tooth pick from his black vest, placing it between his teeth.

"Ha!" Lester interrupted, "If he fixed that entire fence he wouldn't have a bottom line."

The waitress, Alice, around the same age as the table of old timers, walked up with the coffee pot. She knew her regulars like clockwork. After eating, everyone would want one more cup. "Can I fill you boys back up?" she asked, knowing the answer.

Walter, having his back to Alice, turned holding out his mug. "Ever the mind reader. If only my wife had that trait," Walter winked,

as Alice filled the mug and smiled.

"If she did, she would surely leave your

sorry butt," Ben interjected with his own

toothpick marked, smile.

Lester, addressing the whole table, said,

"That's why we have Alice."

Alice smiled as she finished filling the

coffee mugs. These men always put her in a

good mood. "If you boys need anything, I'll be

at the counter."

"Thank you, my dear," Lester said as

Alice made her way back to the counter.

"I'll tell you what I need," Harv said,

continuing the conversation, "Another good

horse."

"You wouldn't know a good horse if he was

standing on your foot," Ben chimed in.

"Like you would either, Ben Brown," Harv

snapped back. "The last time I saw you riding,

you were still on that nag that broke your leg."

Lester rolled his eyes and said, "Neither one of you knows a good horse."

"Oh yeah, aren't you a shopkeeper now?" Ben replied.

"I can out ranch the lot of you and twice on Sunday," Lester said, making his point.

Walter, sipping his coffee, never was one for ribbing his friends. He only spoke up when he had advice or a decent question. "Listen, Harv, if you want a good honest one, you ought to call Sam…" Walter said, stopping when he was met with piercing looks from Ben and Harv.

Knowing what his table mates were up to, Lester said, "Fellers, there's no need for…"

"Rain." Harv interjected, wanting to relieve the tension.

"Rain?" all three questioned in unison.

"Yeah, we need rain," Harv replied, a touch embarrassed now that all three men were looking at him. Ben just shook his head, at the poor attempt to change the subject.

Walter, running his fingers through his crisp combed grey hair, tried another tactic. "Listen Les, are you ever going to start ranching again?"

"I don't know, Walt," Lester said, knowing where the conversation was headed. "There isn't anything for me out there anymore."

"The only reason I ask is because you seem to be spending all your time in town, with your new hardware store and all." Walter said, "If you ever think about selling…"

"Walt," Lester interjected, "I really don't want to talk about it right now."

"Just keep an open mind, that's all I'm…" Walter said but stopped as Lester got up from the table.

From Lester's view, out the window, he saw Sam's pickup park in front of Howard's General Store. "I'm going to have to catch up with you fellers later," Lester said throwing a dollar on the table. He grabbed his coat and headed for the door.

Walter, Harv, and Ben turn in their chairs to peer at what Lester was looking at. Through the café window Sam and Kade could be seen exiting the truck and making their way into the general store.

Chapter 11

Sam and Kade enter the general store together. It's a one room structure with large shelves that help make up five aisles. The place is stock full of food. The Howards used to carry other supplies the community needed, from ranching to mining, but with Lester's hardware store now open, they decided to concentrate on groceries. Fresh fruits and vegetables along with the choicest meats around, provided by the local ranchers.

Wearing a brown apron behind the counter was Barbara Howard. She was tidying up the counter space by stacking jars of fresh strawberry jam. She spotted Sam and Kade in the doorway. "Well, hello boys," she said as they walked up to the front counter.

"Good morning, Barbara," Sam replied.

"Hello, Mrs. Howard," Kade said.

"Did you enjoy the book, Kade?" Barbara asked.

"Yes, ma'am." Kade said with a smile. "I'm ready for another one."

"What do you say?" Sam said, looking at Kade.

"May I please have another book?" Kade said politely correcting himself.

"No problem, sweetheart." Barbara said with a smile. "I'll go in the back and get you a new one."

"Thank you, Barbara. We're going to pick up some things." Sam said.

"Sounds good, I'll be right back," Barbara said as she walked to the back of the store and out the door.

Sam and Kade wandered the aisles, each carrying a basket for their goods. They were filling up on canned beans, corn and peas, bread, condiments, eggs, two pounds of bacon, and some bologna. With their shopping done, they approached the counter just as Barbara re-entered the store with her daughter, Sarah, at her side.

Barbara walked up to Kade and handed him the new book. "Here you go, Kade," Barbara said as nine year old daughter clung to her side. "This book was my favorite when I was your age."

Kade, taking the book, saw it was a copy of J.M. Barrie's *Peter Pan*, enthusiastically said, "Thank you, Mrs. Howard."

"Thank you, Barbara," Sam said as he watched Kade's reaction.

Sarah poked her head around her mother's apron. "Kade, do you remember my daughter, Sarah?" Barbara asked, looking down at her.

Kade brought his gaze up from the book to meet Sarah's blue eyes. "Yes, ma'am" he said. "Hello, Sarah," and tipped his hat slightly.

"Hi, Kade," Sarah said shyly.

* * *

Across Main Street, behind the Sheridan City Café, Lester stood next to his white Cadillac. Arriving a little late this morning, he had been forced to park in the back. He opened the passenger door and reached inside, his hand emerging with a squirming puppy.

The pup was a couple months old, a pretty black tri Australian Shepherd. She had two black floppy ears with a white face. Lester cradled the young dog as he closed the car door and walked away.

***

At the counter, Barbara was ringing up the Murray's purchases. "Looks like it's going to be four dollars and seventy-five cents." She said looking at the register.

"Go ahead, son," Sam said, looking at Kade.

Kade pulled a small wad of cash from his pocket, counting out five one dollar bills. Barbara looked at Sam with curiosity.

"We're working on adding and subtracting," Sam said noticing her interest.

Kade counted the money for a third time, then convinced, handed the bills to Barbara.

She accepted them with a smile, "Thank you, honey."

"How much change will we be getting back?" Sam asked Kade.

Already having the answer locked and loaded Kade quickly said, "Twenty-five cents." Sam nodded his head in approval while Barbara smiled.

"Here you go, sweetheart. A quarter," Barbara said handing the change to a smiling and proud Kade.

"Look, he's already smarter than me," Sam said as he and Barbara laughed. "Thanks again, Barbara."

"No problem, boys." She replied.

Just then, Paul Peterson walked into the store. "Sam, I heard you were over here," Paul said, approaching the counter.

"Hello, Paul," Sam replied as they shook hands.

"Hello, Barbara. You're looking lovely as always," Paul said turning his head her way.

"Good morning, Paul," Barbara replied.

Bending to one knee, Paul looked Kade in his hazel eyes and extended his hand, "Hey there, buckaroo."

"Hi, Mr. Peterson," Kade said, shaking Paul's hand.

"Are you guys still gonna make it to the branding tomorrow?" Paul asked Sam.

"Planning on it," Sam replied. He then turned to Kade, "Son, why don't you haul those groceries out to the truck. I'll be along in a couple of minutes."

Kade nods his head and grabs the groceries Barbara just got done bagging off the counter. Barbara whispered, "I put a couple pieces of candy in there for you," as Kade grabbed the second bag.

"Thank you, Mrs. Howard," Kade said with a toothy smile. He got to the front door and stopped, turned around and said, "Goodbye, Sarah."

"Bye Kade," Sarah said with a smile, leaned up against the front counter.

Stepping off the sidewalk, Kade heads to the back of his dad's pickup. He dropped the tailgate and lifted the grocery bags into the truck. He is interrupted by a voice behind him, "Excuse me, son?" Kade slams the tailgate shut and turns around. Lester stands on the sidewalk holding the puppy.

"Me?" Kade asked.

"Yeah, you. I need your help," Lester said as Kade walks up closer. "Young man, I seem to have a little problem. I found this pup and I don't think I will be able to care for her."

Kade started to pet the puppy on the back of the neck. "What do you want me to do, mister?" Kade asked

"I was wondering if you knew of a good home for this pup?" Lester said. He then cut to the chase, "What I am trying to say is, would you like to take her?"

"Really?!" Kade shouted not hiding his excitement.

"I am just too old son, so if you want her, she's all yours," Lester said handing the puppy to Kade, who quickly hugs the dog. The puppy lick's Kade all over his face.

"Thank you! Thank you, sir!." Kade gratefully said.

"You're very welcome, son." Lester said with a smile.

* * *

Sam opened the driver side door of his pickup and got in. Kade was already in the passenger's seat with the puppy in his lap. Just as Sam was going to start the truck, he noticed the pup. "Kade, where did the dog come from?"

"That man gave her to me," Kade said pointing across the street at Lester.

"Wait here," Sam said eyeballing Lester. He slammed the door as he left the truck.

Sam, with purpose, high-stepped it across the street, getting right in Lester's face.

"What the hell are you trying to pull Les?!" Sam said angrily.

Keeping his composure, Lester said, "I am not trying to pull anything. The pup needed a home."

"I thought my home wasn't good enough, remember?! Find it another home!" Sam shouted as he abruptly turned his back on Lester, storming back to his pickup.

"I don't think it's up to you or me,"
Lester said calmly.

"I told you to stay away," Sam replied,
not turning around.

Getting back to the truck, Sam got in.
Kade was playing with the puppy in his lap. "I
don't want to see you near that man again,
understand?" Sam snapped.

"Yes, sir. I'm sorry," Kade replied.

The Ford fires up and backs out of the
parking spot. Lester watches from the sidewalk
as the truck drives away. Through the
passenger window Kade, his dad unaware, waves
at Lester. Making a small wave in return,
Lester watched as the pickup left the town
quickly behind.

Chapter 12

George was leaning up against the barn day dreaming. The sun, high in the sky, had bathed the ranch in warmth. It was part of the reason he was still in his boxer shorts and boots. The other reason was, he knew he was alone, at least until the horse shoer showed up. He was more worn out than he previously thought and was enjoying the peaceful moment.

The moment was abruptly ended by the backfire of an old beat up pickup rolling quickly into the ranch yard. The truck appeared to be a mixture of three different colors: white, blue, and rust. The color was only diminished by the amount of dents and holes it had. The cherry on top, was the steady stream of black smoke trailing from the back end.

Clicking the engine off, the driver side door opened and Red Burk stepped out. Red was in his late forties and had a hint of ginger, evident mainly in the stubble of his beard. His hair was covered by a hat that looked as old as he was. He wore large brown overalls that helped keep his big belly up and his flask close at hand. George wondered the last time Red had showered.

Taking one last pull of the cigarette, Red put it out on the hood of his truck. He dug into his overall side pocket and pulled out some beechnut chewing tobacco. Taking a handful, he shoved the chew in his mouth.

George watched this spectacle with wide eyes. "You must be Red Burk." George asked.

"Yeah," Red said turning to face George, "Who the hell are you?"

"George, George Goodman," He said standing up straight. "I work here."

Red looked George up and down, and then spat a stream of tobacco. "Well by the looks of you, I hope you're paying Sam and not the other way around." George's bare thin legs had caught Red's attention. "I've seen better legs on a Rhode Island red. That's a chicken, George Goodman." Red explained. "You know what," he said spitting again, "I think I'll call you Chicken. Chicken George."

George just stood there, dumbfounded, and stared at Red. In all his travels he had never met anyone like this.

"Don't just stand there. Let's grab some horses." Red barked. George nodded his head but stood still. "Holy hell Chicken George, grab the halters out of the tack room!"

As if a light went off in his head, George replied, "Right…of course. Do you mind if I get my pants Mr. Red?"

"Sounds like a personal problem to me," Red replied.

George quickly entered the barn and disappeared from view.

"Where you from, Chicken George?" Red asked, yelling into the barn.

"Jersey." George replied from inside the structure.

Red shook his head and spat another stream of chewing tobacco, "nuff said." He replied, grabbing his flask of whiskey.

***

The Murray's pickup truck drove the forty or so miles back to the ranch. Sam was still visibly upset from his interaction with Lester and hadn't said much since leaving town. Likewise, Kade kept to himself, fearing his dad would make him get rid of the dog. At the moment, he was playing with her in his lap.

"What did that man say to you?" Sam asked looking at Kade.

"Nothing, Dad," Kade replied. "He just wanted the puppy to have a good home."

Sam took a deep breath and exhaled. He was not going to let his day be ruined, not by Lester.

"You still want to drive?" Sam asked as his anger subsided.

"Yeah!" Kade cheerfully replied.

Stopping the truck on the side of the road, father and son exited their respective sides. Holding the puppy, Kade meets his dad behind the truck as they switched sides.

"Dad, will you hold her while I drive?" Kade asked, handing the dog over to Sam. After doing so, Kade ran and jumped in the driver side of the pickup. Sam held the puppy and looked at it for a second. All he saw was Lester's face, so he set her in the bed of the truck, walked over and entered the passenger side of the pickup, closing the door.

A couple miles down the road, after Kade got the gas pedal under control, the pickup truck passed a prison chain gang working on the highway. There were ten inmates on each side of the road wearing striped jumpsuits. The fat-bellied warden, wearing mirrored sunglasses, sat atop his horse with a double barreled shotgun.

Kade slowed the truck, at his dad's instruction, to pass the prison work at a safe speed. Sam gazed out his window and made eye contact with two of the rougher looking inmates. Their skin was like leather and their eyes squinted from the sun. They were close enough to the pickup that Sam could read the names on their sweat stained jumpsuits: Charlie and Frank.

* * *

Returning home, Kade stood next to the pickup holding his new puppy as his dad, carrying the grocery bags, walked around to meet him.

"Dad, Mr. Red is here," Kade said as he noticed Red's one of a kind truck parked by the barn.

"Yep," Sam replied, "Why don't you get the groceries to the house, I'll go see what Red and George are up too."

Kade nodded his head as his dad handed him the bags. Kade carried the grocery bags and the pup to the ranch house as Sam made his way to the barn.

Entering the barn, Sam found Red sitting in a chair taking a pull from his whiskey flask.

"Working hard as usual," Sam said as Red finished and offered the flask. "Haven't touched the stuff in years."

"I know it," Red said, "but no one likes a God damn quitter."

Shaking his head Sam replied, "Did they give you any trouble?"

"The horses, hell no," Red said, "Now your hired man on the other hand, he's a hand full."

"Where is George?" Sam asked a touch concerned, which surprised him. Red pointed to a stall in the back of the barn, where the sound of gagging could be heard. "What did you do?"

"He wants to be a cowboy, I gave him some beechnut," Red said with a smirk. George, fully clothed, emerged from the horse stall wiping his chin. "There he is, Chicken George. I call him Chicken. Have you seen his legs?" Red said, turning to Sam.

"George, do not listen to him. Are you alright?" Sam asked.

"Never better," George said, clearing his throat. "Cowboy Red has some really good stories. He's a real cowboy, isn't he?"

"Red has some pretty good stories, but that's what they are, just stories," Sam replied, shooting a look at Red.

"Come on, Sam." Red said.

"Come on, Red. You know you can be full of shit sometimes." Sam chimed back.

"Hey, with this hired hand of yours I got a new audience," Red said, taking another drink of whiskey.

"I see you're drinking as much as ever." Sam said, "have you cut back on smoking?"

"I used to just smoke after sex, now it's pretty much all the time," Red said with a smile.

Sam noticed Kade entering the barn with his new puppy, "Here comes Kade and his new pup, keep it clean." Sam turned to face his son, "Did you get the groceries put away?"

"Yes, sir" Kade said proudly, "and I threw out that old milk. You know it had chunks in it?"

George caught himself from throwing up and ran back to the horse stall. Red roared with a belly laugh and slapped his knee.

"What did I say?" Kade asked confused. Puking could be heard from the back of the barn again. "What's wrong with Mr. Goodman?"

"You mean Chicken George," Red interjected, "have you seen his legs?"

"No, sir," Kade replied.

"Well, I've seen better legs on a rooster," Red explained.

Shaking his head at Red's comment, Sam watched George slowly re-enter the breezeway and lean on a wall. "How many did you do today Red?"

"I think I did four shoes and three trims," Red replied.

Red had always been a hard worker, when he wanted to be, but he wasn't afraid to cut a few corners. Sam knew this and always wanted a second opinion, one of the reasons he left George there. "George how many did he do?" he asked.

George, getting his bearings back replied, "I think it was three shoes and four trims."

Nodding his head Sam said, "So what do we owe you Red?"

"It's five a shoe and a dollar a trim," Red said. "You know I ain't good with math. Kade, what do you think?"

Kade loved it when someone, other than his dad, brought him into a grown up conversation. Not wanting to disappoint, he quickly replied, "Nineteen dollars."

"Are you sure?" Red said, scratching his head.

"He's right," George interjected. One thing he knew was how to ring up a sale.

Sam pulled out a twenty dollar bill and paid Red.

"Thank you," Red said, "I was gonna do a couple more but I got to drinking. I know you don't like it when I get their feet crooked."

"I appreciate that," Sam said with a smile, "That's why you still work here." Sam started to walk out of the barn. Kade, holding the new pup, joined his father.

"Nice pup Kade," Red said.

Turning back to look at Red, Kade replied, "Thank you Mr. Red."

"Son, go put the dog at the house, we need to visit your mom." Kade waved to Red and exited the barn. Sam turns and looks at George, still leaning on the barn wall, "George…"

"I know, the works over there?" George chimed in as Red smiled at the statement.

"No, pick up the halters please." Sam walked out of the barn and said, "Always a pleasure, Red."

Chapter 13

Sam and Kade stand over Emmie's grave,
with the sunset at their backs. The large tree
she was buried under has gotten even bigger,
providing much shade during a bright and sunny
day. Both father and son have removed their
hats. The quiet moment helped Sam wash away
the troubles of the day, as he stood here with
his family.

"Son, why don't you grab some flowers for
your mom," Sam said pointing at some
wildflowers growing in the tall grass. Kade

smiled and walked over to where his father was pointing, about ten feet away. Sam kneels down when Kade is far enough away and whispers to his wife, "Sweetheart, you would be so proud of Kade. I'm doing my best, but I think he's growing up the way you wanted." Sam started to tear up. "He says his prayers, so polite and respectful. Not to mention the best little cowboy around." Sam paused as he closed his eyes, "God, I miss you so much."

Kade came back with the freshly picked wildflowers. Sam stood up wiping the tears from his eyes. "Those look great, good job, son. You know, the last thing I said to your mom was that I needed her. I still do. I ask her for guidance all the time."

Kade smiled up at his dad. He loved hearing stories about Emmie. "I love you, mom" Kade said as he placed the flowers next to his mother's cross. Standing back up, Sam gave him a hug.

With his arm around Kade's shoulders, Sam said, "Lord, it is through Your amazing grace and incredible love that I am who I am. A sinner saved by grace through faith, in the love of our Lord and Saviour."

The prayer was capped with an "Amen" from both father and son. Hats in hand, they turned and walked back to the ranch house, Sam still with his arm around Kade.

The young pup was sleeping on the porch when the sound of footsteps, walking up the steps, woke her. She was met with a smiling Kade who enthusiastically started to pet her. Sam opened the front door and entered with Kade behind him, the puppy followed.

* * *

Kade, having already been tucked in, was lying in his bed. Sam leaned in the doorway,

"Get some sleep cowboy, we got a big day ahead of us tomorrow." He turned out the light and began to leave the bedroom.

"Dad," Kade said as his father was leaving, "I think I'm going to name the puppy Grace."

Sam stopped and smiled, "Grace is a good name." After a short pause he continued, "Now get some sleep, son." Sam left the bedroom, closing the door behind him.

He walked into the living room, where George was lying on the couch. Not eating supper because of his tobacco incident, Sam cut George some slack, not to mention putting up with Red. Sam went to his chair and sat down. Removing his boots, he leaned back in the chair. It wasn't long before the pup, Grace, was at his feet looking at him.

"If you're gonna be living here, you got to pull your own weight," Sam said as he looked at Grace. "Just ask George."

Hearing his name, George sat up on the couch. "Mr. Murray, does this ever get any easier?" he asked.

"No," Sam said with a smirk, "but it does get tolerable."

George nodded his head and made his way to the front door. "Night." He said as he exited the house.

"Get some rest, George," Sam said, as George closed the front door. Since it was just Grace and Sam now, she tried to jump in his lap. "No, stay down," he said pushing her off him. "I think your lessons ought to start right now." Sam placed Grace in a sitting position, "Grace, sit down."

As soon as Sam's hands were off of Grace, the puppy stood back up looking at him. Sam shook his head and forcefully said "Grace, sit down." The puppy tilted her head, paused, and then sat down like she had just been taught.

Surprised at his dog training abilities, Sam looked at Grace, "Well, you might work out after all."

Chapter 14

The Peterson Ranch was located southwest
of the Murray property. It was a sprawling
piece of land that was three times the acreage
and had been in the Peterson family for over a
hundred years. Paul's grandfather started it
and over the century that followed his father
had expanded it until it was Paul's turn to
take over. It was the largest ranch in the
county and ran the most head of cattle by far.

When it came to branding, the Peterson's
always turned it into an event, with plenty of

food and drink. The amount of cattle they raised was too much for just their hired hands to brand in one day. Having the branding on the county social calendar all but assured their neighbors would show up and help. It was also a day to show off your cowboying skills and any new horse someone wanted to sell.

A large herd, over three hundred cows and calves, are being rounded up by ten cowboys. Kade is riding next to his dad, taking instruction, as the two push thirty head into the larger herd. Kade, riding Pard, moves around the cattle with the ease of a much older cowboy. The skill does not escape the view of Paul.

"I got to hand it to you, Sam," Paul said, riding alongside him. "That boy of yours is quite a hand."

"He listens and is full of try," Sam replied, watching Kade work. This was the first Peterson branding Sam and Kade could work together, Kade having reached the age Sam could trust him on his own.

"We'll get these critters corralled and separate the calves," Paul said. "Then the fun will start."

Sam turned back to Paul and said with a smile, "Wait till you see him rope."

***

The large herd had been separated with the cows in a holding pen while the calves were in the branding pen. Sam, on foot, stood next to Kade on Pard. Kade was looking at the calf herd and felt overwhelmed.

"Now just ride into the calves and rope one," Sam said trying to simplify the task and calm Kade's nerves. "Drag 'em back over to me and I'll brand 'em." Kade answered by nervously nodding his head. "Don't worry son, Pard will help you."

A pushy young cowhand, Cody, almost twice Kade's age, bullies his way past, bumping into Kade and Pard. "Out of my way, kid," he said as he pulled his rope out and rode into the herd of calves.

Kade seemed stunned by the altercation. "Don't worry about it," Sam said. To help Kade forget, he slapped Pard on the butt propelling the horse forward. "Now, get to work." Sam stood next to the fire ring, heating the branding irons, as Kade rode into the herd.

What happened next Sam would re-tell proudly for years, to anyone who would listen: the youngest cowboy in the pen roped the most calves. Kade missed with his first loop and after a snide smirk from Cody, he got in the zone. His rope never missed its mark the rest of the day. He and Pard were bringing calves to his dad faster than Sam could keep the branding iron hot.

Outside the branding pen, Red and George sat on the tailgate of Red's one of a kind pickup.

"How come you ain't helping Red?" George asked, watching the cowboys in the branding pen.

Taking a sip from his whiskey flask, Red replied, "I've been drinking and I'm past the go get'em stage. I've branded thousands of em'." Red offered the flask to George. "Chicken George, let me ask you something. You ever had calf fries?"

"What are calf fries?" George asked, taking a pull from the flask.

"I thought you were in the deli business," Red said, taking his flask back. He then pointed into the branding pen, "You see those nuts their cutting out of those calves. Fried up there ain't nothing like' em."

With Red talking about the deli business, it seemed like the perfect opportunity for George to bring up something he had been thinking about. "You know Red, I've been thinking of opening up a deli in town. What do you think?" He asked.

"Every cowboy needs a good sandwich, now and then." Red replied. "You're already quitting Sam?"

"No… well maybe, I don't know. It's just something I was thinking about," George explained.

Red nodded his head, "If you do, be sure to put those calf fries on the menu. Little sauerkraut and mustard and name it after me. It'll knock your hat in the creek," Red said with a smile.

* * *

All the cowboys were gathered around a table in the branding pen drinking ice-cold lemonade. With the work done, and the unmistakable smell of burnt cowhide lingering, the men spoke about the condition of the cattle and the generosity of the Peterson's. But what most of the cowboys talked about was the skill of young Kade Murray. When there were only a handful of calves left to brand, everyone backed off and watched Kade and Pard work. Frustration was painted all over Cody's face as he was told to quit. He was out roped and out worked by a kid half his age.

Kade was enjoying his glass of lemonade as Paul approached him, "Son, you are one hell of a cowboy," he said with a grin. "If you ever get tired of your old man, I will always have a place for you."

"Thank you, Mr. Peterson." Kade replied almost feeling embarrassed by the compliment.

"He's still got a lot to learn," Sam chimed in.

Cody came to the table and pushed his way into the crowd of cowboys, again bumping into Kade. This time, Kade had enough and turned to confront Cody.

"Just what do you think you're doing?" Sam asked as he stepped in front of Kade.

"I am tired of him pushing me around," Kade said.

Sam takes Kade to the side. "Son, you have already bested him. Everyone here saw it. A fight is exactly what he's looking for. Don't give him the satisfaction." Looking Kade in the eyes, Sam continued, "Nothing good ever comes from losing your temper. Trust me on that."

"But, Dad…" Kade replied, not convinced.

"Trust me, son." Sam said as Cody started to walk towards Kade. "I think that's enough for today," He continued as he stepped between the boys. Cody stopped, his eyes drifted from

129

Kade to Sam. He gulped his cup of lemonade, turned and walked away.

"Can I talk you into staying for supper?" Paul asked as he passed Cody.

"Thanks for the offer but we still have work to do back home."

"I can understand that. Thanks again for all your help." Paul said, shaking Sam's hand.

"No problem, it was our pleasure." Sam said.

"You too, buckaroo," Paul said shaking Kade's hand as well.

Exiting the branding pen, Sam noticed George loafing with Red. "George, let's go. The work's over here."

Chapter 15

The Murray's pickup, pulling a two horse trailer, entered the ranch yard at dusk, and came to a stop next to the barn. Kade was the last to get out because he was sitting in the middle of the bench seat. His dad had already untied their horses and was unloading them, by the time Kade got to the horse trailer.

"Be sure to grain them good," Sam said handing the lead ropes to Kade. "They worked hard today." Kade nodded his head and led Pard and his father's horse into the barn. "George and I will get the feed ready for the rest of the herd," Sam explained as Kade disappeared into the barn. George quickly accompanied Sam as he walked to the haystack.

★★★

The Ford pickup truck bounced around finding a path through one of the Murray's pastures. This time it was not pulling a trailer but the back was filled with ten bales of hay. Sam drove with Kade in the passenger seat while George sat on the hay in the back.

"You see son, if we leave some feed for these horses, they will be easier to catch tomorrow," Sam said stopping the truck. "You drive while George and I throw the hay out."

"Yes, sir." Kade said with a grin and thinking to himself, this is new. Usually he would be in the bed of the truck, it is nice having George around.

Sam exits the pickup and jumps into the bed with George and the hay. Kade slid across the seat to the steering wheel.

"Ok son, just keep us right alongside the fence," Sam explained.

Kade rolled the truck along slowly, giving his dad and George time to throw the bales out. Every fifty feet or so, Sam could cut a bale open and he and George would kick it out of the pickup. Hitting the ground the hay would explode into a large area, making sure every critter would get a bite to eat.

"Kade," Sam said, "If two plus two is four, then what is two times two?" Sam was trying to make conversation during the mundane task.

"Is this multiplication?" Kade asked from the cab of the truck.

"Yes, we've talked about it," Sam replied. "Try and picture the problem in your head."

Kade took his father's advice, but in doing so, he forgot about the fence, which he crashed straight through. He stopped the pickup and jumped out with a frightened look on his face.

"Kade, you alright?" Sam said, startled himself. "George?"

"Yes…I'm sorry, Dad," Kade replied.

"I'm good," George said as well.

Thankful everyone was alright, Sam could continue, "Sorry is not going to fix it. Grab the pliers out of the glove box."

The pickup was parked next to the hole in the fence. George was pulling the barbed wire tight as a kneeling Sam clipped the wire in place and Kade held the fence post in place.

"Son, it's not that hard. If two plus two is four, then what is two times two?" Sam asked, not letting Kade give up on the problem. "Pull it tight, George." Kade furrowed his brow thinking as George bared down on the wire. "Remember, it's two, two times." Sam said as he tried to help Kade.

"Four?" Kade said unsure.

Sam, admiring the repaired fence, stood back up, putting his hand on Kade's shoulder. "Good, now hopefully you won't have to break something every time you learn a lesson."

* * *

Dusk had faded and night was coming on when Sam and Kade headed for the ranch house. Grace ran off the porch to greet them and excitedly began jumping all over Kade.

"Don't let Grace get away with that." Sam said. "Teach her some manners, make her sit." Kade looked at his dad. "Go on."

Kade, knowing all his dad's lessons are connected, gestures with his hand. The same way he worked with Pard. "Sit down, Grace," Kade said with authority.

Grace sat right down, to the surprise of both Kade and Sam.

"Smart dog," Sam explained.

* * *

Ten minutes later, Kade holding a sandwich in one hand, exits the house.

"Tell George that's the best we got. This ain't the Five Star Deli," Sam said from the doorway.

"Yes, sir." Kade replied and looked down at the plain bologna sandwich.

Sam closed the door but not before Grace snuck out and followed Kade down the porch steps. The pair made their way towards the barn. Grace tries to take a bite of the sandwich, so Kade held it higher.

George was sitting on his bunk with his boots off when Kade and Grace entered his barn room.

"Hey, Mr. Goodman," Kade said holding out the sandwich. "My dad said this is the best we got."

George looked at the sandwich, and then reluctantly took it from Kade. Grace, licked her lips, watching the exchange.

"I think I finally found something your dad's not good at," George said as he eyeballed the sandwich. Kade looked at him with curiosity. "It may not seem like much to you, kid. But a good sandwich can make the worst day livable. That's one thing my time at the Five Star taught me."

George spotted Grace staring at the sandwich. He tossed it to her and she immediately started to gobble it up. "Well, your dad's creation has at least one fan."

"What's it like?" Kade asked still looking at George.

"The Five Star Deli?" George replied.

"Other places." Kade said. "All I know is this ranch. I've never been anywhere else, except for going into town."

George saw the sincerity in Kade's eyes and said, "Take it from me kid, you don't need to. I've been to a lot of places. None compare to here. Buildings reaching to the sky, so many people and cars it's hard to breathe."

"Is that why you left, Mr. Goodman?" Kade asked.

"I'm looking for what you and your dad have," George said.

"A ranch of your own?" Kade replied.

"A home," George said, lying back down on his bunk. "I don't want your dad upset with me, so you better run off to bed."

Nodding his head Kade said, "Goodnight, Mr. Goodman," and he turned to leave.

"Night, kid." George said.

Kade stepped through the doorway then stopped. He turned around and said, "Mr. Goodman, I'm glad you found your way here."

George smiled as Kade and Grace exited his room. This was the first bit of validation he had received in a long time. It may have come from an eight year old boy, but Kade was better than any cowboy he had read about.

Chapter 16

Morning found Sam, Kade, and George sitting around the breakfast table. All the stock had been fed, so now it was their turn to sit down and eat before the rest of the day started. Grace sat at Kade's feet nibbling on pieces of bacon he snuck her under the table.

"Are you ready to have some fun today?" Sam said leaning back from his plate of bacon and eggs and looking at Kade.

"You bet," Kade enthusiastically replied.

"Running horses is nothing like trailing cows," Sam explained with a grin. "It's one of my favorite things to do." Kade nodded in agreement while George nervously sipped his cup of coffee. "Sorry, George, this is a two man job," he said turning towards George. "So, I'd like you to start cleaning the tack room."

"No problem, Mr. Murray," George said, looking relieved. He took a pause and then decided to take a chance. "Have you ever had a good deli sandwich?"

"What are you trying to say?" Sam asked looking right at George. "My sandwich wasn't to your liking?"

"I don't know, you're going to have to ask the dog," George replied with a smirk.

Sam rolled his eyes and said. "If you must know, my wife Emmie used to make the best sandwich I ever had."

"And what kind of sandwich was that?" George asked with curiosity.

Kade smiled, loving to hear new stories about his mom, as his dad sat back in his chair and said, "Roast beef, a little mustard, pickles, thin sliced tomatoes, and some nice purple onions." There wasn't a thing Sam did not remember about Emmie. "George, there was nothing better. Why do you ask?"

"Now that's what I'm talking about," George replied with a big smile. "What do you think about a deli in town?"

"You thinking of quitting?" Sam asked reading more into the question.

"No," George quickly replied, "no, just making conversation. I'll get to work on the tack room."

"Sounds good," Sam said, turning his attention to Kade. "Son, why don't you bring Grace along today?"

"Do you mean it?" Kade asked surprised.

"She may be of some help. You just keep an eye on her and tell her what to do," Sam said as he tossed Grace a strip of bacon.

* * *

Sam and Kade are riding through the tall grass with Grace bouncing behind Pard.

"When we get the horses into a herd, I'll take the lead mare and you follow behind," Sam explained, "We're gonna be moving fast, let Pard run. I'll lead the horses back to the corrals. All you have to do is keep them moving." Sam looked down at Grace, "Let Grace help you, but watch her. Don't let her scatter the herd."

"Yes, sir," Kade replied with a serious look.

"And don't forget to have fun," Sam said with a smile, noticing Kade's seriousness.

It took a fair amount of time, but Sam
and Kade got the horses rounded up. They had
fifty head grazing in a large valley. Father
and son overlooked them from a hilltop,
searching for any strays. Turning, Kade
spotted a loan colt on the backside of the
hill.

"Dad, I see one!" Kade blurted out as he
wheeled Pard in that direction, disturbing
Grace who was lying at Pard's feet. The colt
was a roan with a large scar on its left
shoulder, more than likely from crashing
through a fence.

Before Sam could tell him to leave it,
Kade began running Pard down the hill after
the roan colt. But before Kade makes it even
twenty feet or so, Sam cut him off, bringing
him to a stop.

"Don't you ever run your horse downhill!" Sam shouted, "I have told you before and I will not tell you again!"

"But, Dad!" Kade explained, watching the roan horse run in the opposite direction. "The colt! He's getting away!"

"I don't care. No horse is worth your safety. I want you to remember that," Sam said with authority. "Now, promise me you will never do that again."

"Yes, sir," Kade said, lowering his gaze and not looking his dad in the eyes.

"Kade, promise me."

Raising his head to look his father in the eye, "I promise," Kade replied.

"Thank you," Sam said. Turning towards the herd of horses, he continued, "Now, let's have some fun."

***

Standing in front of the tack room, with an intense stare, was George. He reached into his pocket and pulled out his own pouch of beechnut chewing tobacco. Taking a pinch, he put some in his mouth. Staring at the door jam, "You ain't getting me today," he said as he spat.

Carefully, he ducked his head and entered the tack room. Assessing the situation, George decided to start with the saddles. Picking the first one up, he turned quickly to exit, smashing his head into the doorway header. His toes, pointed up, were hanging out the tack room door as he lay on his back, knocked out.

***

Circling the horses, Sam and Kade keep them in a tight herd. Like clockwork, the lead mare, pinning her ears, found a hole and starts running. Immediately, Sam accelerates his horse to her shoulder and matches the mare stride for stride. The herd strings out and follows, four horses wide, at a fast pace. Swinging his rope at the back of the herd, Kade pushes the big stud horse, who in turn bulldozes the horses forward.

The pastures of the Murray Ranch are turned into a race track as the horses rumble through the open land. Kade keeps the horses moving as his dad steers them in the right direction. The trampled grass of where the herd had just been is followed by Grace, trying her best to keep up.

"Yeeeehaaaaa!" Kade screams as he lets Pard run as fast as he can. The shout of excitement had Sam smiling as he looked back at Kade.

Sam had the fast running herd on a beeline for the biggest holding pen. As soon as the lead mare blasted through the gate opening, Sam slowed his horse, "Push'em hard, son!"

Kade kicked a sweat stained Pard into another gear as his dad dismounted next to the gate. The fast running herd followed the lead mare right into the large corral with Kade driving them hard. Sam dropped the latch on the gate as the stud horse thundered through. Kade pulled rein right next to his dad.

"Way to go, cowboy," Sam proudly said.

"That was so great!" Kade, with a huge smile, shouted.

"I told you," Sam replied.

Grace, panting hard, finally caught up as father and son admired their herd.

Chapter 17

Mid-morning found the ranch yard quiet and peaceful. The herd of horses were milling around and grazing on hay Sam had George throw into the large corral. Having something to eat always helped a new herd transition from the pasture to an arena. They would be concentrated on their bellies and not kicking, fighting, or tearing a hole in the fence.

In front of the tack room, Kade was once again trying to master the butterfly rope trick. George sat on a bucket in the breezeway reading one of his western books. His hat was on the ground next to him, because it hurt to wear it. His forehead was sporting a large red mark.

Swinging his rope fast, Kade let the loop go and then rolled his wrist, getting the loop to dance around him. His eyes got wide while his smile reached from ear to ear. "Dad!" Kade shouted into the tack room, "Dad, I did it! I finally did it!"

Sam, framed in the tack room doorway, had his bronc riding gear on. His spurs jingled as he walked out; these spurs had rowels meant for getting a hold of a critter's hide. He carried his bronc saddle, a normal stock saddle with the horn removed. He held it from the back of the swells, on his right hip over his brown batwing chaps.

"I told you, you'd get it," Sam said as he saw the look of accomplishment all over Kade's face.

"Watch." Kade, with confidence this time, started the trick over. Once again, he had the loop doing exactly what he wanted. George looked up from his book to check the rope trick out; he clapped upon watching.

"Not bad," Sam said watching his son dance with the rope, "now go get Pard. We got a job ahead of us."

Kade, having finished, drops his rope and nods in agreement. He runs past George. Grace, lying next to the tack room door, jumped up and followed.

"How's the head George?" Sam asked, turning towards George. George rubbed his wound and feeling embarrassed, had nothing to say. "Come on down to the arena," Sam said

gesturing with his head, "You'll learn
something those books will never teach you."

***

Sam sat on the top rail of the pole
corral looking at the herd of horses. He was
going over which ones were keepers and which
one might put a black mark on their reputation
for solid mounts. It wasn't long until he was
joined by Kade, riding Pard alongside the
fence.

"The Northcott family wants five horses.
We need to pick the five best." Sam said.

Kade scans the herd himself, "Well, how
about that one, the bay gelding?" He was
pointing at a beautiful brown horse with
excellent confirmation and a long mane and
tail.

Sam smiles, "Yeah, and those four behind
him." Getting down from the fence he was
pleased Kade was acquiring a good eye for

horses. "Cut those five horses out, and into the round pen. I'll fetch my rope."

George made his way down from the barn and stood back watching from a safe distance. Sam opened the gate to the corral allowing Kade and Pard to enter. Riding through the gate, Grace followed.

"Make sure she minds you." Sam said, watching Grace sneak into the arena.

"Yes, sir," Kade replied. "Come on, Grace."

Kade rode into the herd, maneuvering Pard around the horses and cutting the five they wanted to the side. With his rope in hand, Sam opened the gate to the round pen. Kade, with a little help from Grace, pushed the five horses into the smaller corral. Sam closed the gate behind them.

"I like your pick, let's start with the bay," Sam said opening a small gate in the

153

round pen. Knowing his job, Kade pushed the other four horses through the small gate and into a holding pen. Once done, the round pen held Kade and Pard, Sam, and the wild young bay horse.

George, watching the action, had to get a better look. He was now on the outside of the round pen peering through the wood slats. He could see Sam in the middle of the arena swinging his rope, as the bay horse ran circles around him. When the right moment happened, Sam tossed his loop. The rope settled around the neck of the gelding as Sam pulled it tight.

The horse, feeling the foreign object around its neck pulled back, dragging Sam forward as he planted his boots in the dirt. Not wanting the horse to choke, Sam quickly threw a coil of rope over the bay horse' nose, making a makeshift halter. If the horse pulled now, the pressure would be on the bridge of his nose and not his windpipe.

Sam gestured with his head and Kade rides Pard up and grabs the rope, dallying the rope to his saddle horn. Feeling pressure again, the bay gelding throws a fit, jumping and flopping around. The tantrum is short lived because Kade and Pard hold steady pressure, causing the horse to stand still.

Sam grabbed a halter with a long thick rein that was lying in the seat of his bronc saddle. "Go ahead and move him around a bit," he instructed.

Kade, with the rope dallied to the horn, urges Pard forward. They start making circles with the young bay gelding following. Each round they make Kade brings the gelding closer by re-dallying and taking the slack out of the rope, until finally the bay horse's head is next to Kade's leg.

"Easy, easy," Kade said talking to the young horse.

"Good," Sam said approaching Kade with the halter. "Now, gently, see if you can slip the halter on him."

"Take it easy, buddy," Kade said as he gently slipped the halter over the bay horse's nose and latched it. "There, that wasn't so bad, was it?" He continued, removing his father's rope.

"Good job, son," Sam said watching. "Now keep him moving while I grab my saddle."

Kade moves the bay horse around using the long rein from his dad's bronc halter. When Sam approaches, carrying the saddle, Kade dallies up and stops the young gelding.

"Take it easy, Bay," Sam said, "Take it easy. Keep talking to him, son."

"Easy," Kade said listening to his father's instructions, "you're alright. Easy."

Sam cautiously and calmly saddles the young bay gelding. When he feels the cinch, the bay horse jumps and pulls back on the bronc rein. Sam steps to the side as Kade and Pard put a stop to it. When the coast is clear, Sam re-approaches the gelding and pulls the cinch tight. The horse does not move.

"Alright, are you ready?" Sam asked looking at Kade.

With a determined face Kade replied, "Yes, sir."

Sam pulled his hat down tight and slapped his hands on the inside of his thighs, the sound that his chaps made and the feel of the impact got his adrenaline flowing. He then, not to spook the gelding, very slowly, crawls onto the back of Pard, "Good boy, Pard." Sam now sat right behind Kade and the cantle of his saddle. "Ok, son, bring him close and tight."

Kade nudges Pard with his left spur and the horse side steps right alongside the bay bronc. Taking the slack out of the rein, Kade dallies tighter as Pard crowds up against the young horse.

Pleased with the situation and placing his hand on Kade's shoulder, Sam said, "Here we go." He leap frogged from Pard to his bronc saddle, causing the young gelding, having felt the new weight, to throw his head and move around. "Easy, easy," Sam said, getting his seat and squeezing the swells with his chaps.

Kade handed the bronc rein over to his father but kept hold of the halter. The young gelding had his head in Kade's lap, still thinking he was held tight to Pard.

Sam rolled his hips forward, getting a deep seat in his bronc saddle and said, "All right, turn him loose!"

Kade let go of the halter and wheeled Pard quickly out of the way. Finally having his head free from restraint, the bay gelding lunges forward and jumps in the air with all four legs. The height of the leap had Sam's upper body above the top rail of the round pen. Seeing that, George had to get a better view. He crawled to the top rail and draped his arms over to watch.

The gelding hit the ground with his front feet and kicked at the sun with his hind end. Sam drove his spurs forward and lifted on the rein to keep his butt in the saddle. With dust flying, the horse ducked left, then hard right, kicking over his head. Sam matched the young bronc move for move. As the horse jumped and crested into another kick, Sam would bring his body ahead then drive his hips forward as they would come to the ground.

Kade, next to the fence of the arena, watched in awe the way his father rode with ease. Likewise, George was amazed at what he was witnessing: his own personal rodeo. The young bay horse had a lot of try, but soon realized he would not shake his sticky rider. Throwing his head up, and dripping sweat, the gelding went from bucking into a nice gallop.

Sam rode the horse in circles until he was sure he was in charge. When the horse blew his nostrils he heard what he was waiting for. He brought the bay gelding into a tight circle until he stopped. Then, very calmly and easy, Sam dismounted and pet the young horse on the neck. "Well," Sam said looking at his audience, "only four more." Kade smiled with excitement as George gave two thumbs up.

After lunch, the afternoon was filled with the sounds and smells of leather, sweat, and true grit. Kade and Pard did their job readying the remaining four horses with ropes and bronc reins. Sam, like a dime novel hero tried, tested and conquered each bronc with ease and determination. George watched the show with a mixture of respect and self-doubt.

Crawling off the last horse, Sam stretched his sore body and looked at Kade. "In a couple years, this job is all yours."

Kade smiled, and said, "Yes, sir."

Chapter 18

Sam and George sat on the porch while
Kade played with Grace, watching the evening
sunset begin. It was a nice way to end the
day, overlooking the property they work so
hard for. Sam sat and let his muscles relax
knowing a good night's rest would re-charge
his batteries.

George had been unusually quiet since the
round pen. When asked 'if he was ok?' he just
responded with 'I'm just thinking.' He turned

to Sam and said, "Mr. Murray, that was amazing what you did today."

"Thank you, George, but it was a team effort," Sam replied with a smile.

"Watching you out there," George paused and looked out at the ranch. Turning back to Sam, he continued, "I got no business trying to be a cowboy."

"What makes you say that?" Sam asked noticing the stark contrast from the day George arrived.

"You make it look so easy and I…" George stops because the phone can be heard ringing.

Sam gets up from his chair, patting George on the back, "Hold that thought," and entered the house.

George turned to Kade, "Hey, kid," Kade looked at George. "That dad of yours is the real deal. You watch and learn. You're already a better cowboy than anyone I've read about."

"Thank you, Mr. Goodman," Kade replied with a smile, "I will."

Sam walked back on the porch with a curious look on his face, "George, it's for you, it's Red."

George jumped out of his chair and quickly went inside.

* * *

Not being able to stay idle for too long, Sam had moved down to the barn and started to organize the tack room. Kade took the opportunity to continue practicing his rope tricks. George entered the barn and stood outside the tack room.

Sam saw George and said, "George, tomorrow we really have to get this place cleaned up." He noticed the somber look on George's face. "Is everything alright? What did Red want with you?"

"Look, Sam," George said seriously, "I am sorry to admit this but I may have overestimated my cowboying abilities."

Kade stopped his rope trick and looked at his father. They both knew he had grossly overestimated, but to hear him say it was another story.

"George," Sam said trying to ease the tension, "it's just a tack room to clean out."

Shaking his head, George gave the tack room door a death stare, "That tack room is a whole other story." Looking at the ground, George continued, "No, it's this cowboy job. It's not all latigos and lace like in the novels." Sam and Kade stared at him with curiosity. "Listen, I appreciate everything you guys have done for me." George raises his head and looks at Sam, "I should be reading about cowboys, not trying to be one."

"George, it takes time…" Sam interjected but was cut off.

"You said yourself, you don't buy spurs, you earn them," George paused, and then continued, "Red's coming to pick me up and take me into town."

"George, whether you want to work here or not, we'd have given you a ride to town," Sam said.

"I know you would. But I got myself here, I should get myself out," George replied. Not waiting for a response, he walked back to his bunk to gather his belongings. Sam and Kade stood, shocked.

* * *

Red sat in his pickup truck with the driver's side window down. The back fire upon his arrival alerted Sam and Kade he had rolled into the ranch yard. They stood next to the truck as George emerged from the barn carrying his duffel bag.

"Did you grab everything?" Sam asked, "Don't forget your spurs."

"I got' em. I know I didn't earn them, but I got' em." He turned back and looked at the barn. "I thought I was cut out for ranching but I guess I wasn't sewed up right." He turned and walked to Red's truck, throwing his duffel in the back.

"You gonna be alright, George?" Sam asked sincerely.

"I'm gonna move into town and see if I can get some type of work that's not so livestock oriented." He paused and smiled, "Maybe something with pastrami." Kade ran over and hugged him, George paused at the unexpected gesture, then hugged him back. "I'm gonna find my home," George whispered to Kade. He was visibly sad, but Kade managed a smile.

"You're burning daylight, Chicken!" Red blurted from the pickup.

George opened the passenger side door and said, "Sam, Kade. Thank you. For everything. I know I didn't deserve the chance but I sure appreciate it."

"Take care, George," Sam replied, and then turned, "Red."

"Glad you got to see me," Red chimed in with a tobacco filled grin.

"Bye, Mr. Goodman, Mr. Red," Kade said.

The truck started up and drove out of the ranch yard with its familiar trail of black smoke.

"You gonna miss him?" Sam asked. Kade replied with a head nod. "For some odd reason, I believe I will too. Don't worry, I doubt that's the last we've seen of ol' George. He sure does leave an impression," Sam smiled, "kind of like the path of a tornado."

As early evening settled on the ranch, father and son watched the one working taillight of Red's truck disappear into the distance.

Chapter 19

1962.

Dust is rising from the round pen again
on a cloudless hot day. There is no breeze and
the afternoon heat hung in the air. The arena
showed the years of use, with a few poles and
wood slates having been replaced. Being a
vital link in the Murray's chain of producing
the best horses in the territory, Sam insists
on having the round pen in good, if not great,
shape for the safety of him, Kade, and their
horses.

As always, Pard stood in the corner, out of the way, after his job was done. But for the first time in the history of the young Murray Ranch, Sam, with a salt and pepper mustache, sat on Pard watching a spectacular bronc ride. He was not sitting still, much to the discomfort of Pard. Sam was watching a young sorrel horse buck and making the counter moves. It was like second nature, but this time his adrenaline was pumping as a teacher and father. "Don't weaken, son! You've got 'em!"

Kade sat atop the young bronc, the spitting image of his father. Not only because he was wearing Sam's bronc riding gear, but now, sixteen years old, he had begun to look like him as well. The young sorrel would crest into a jump and, before he could hit the ground, Sam would yell, "Drive to the front end!"

Whether it was second nature or that his father was always a step ahead of the horses, Kade drove his hips and spurs forward, having his body in the right position before the sorrel hit the ground and kicked.

"That-a boy!" Sam cheered, watching the bronc bound into another jump. He was amazed and proud of his son's effort. 'This ranch was going to last for a long time' he thought to himself.

Kade, looking like the Wyoming license plate image, rode the young sorrel horse to a stand-still. He urged the bronc forward with his spurs and had him loping around the pen. After a few circles, Kade brought the horse to a stop.

Calmly dismounting, Kade smiled and looked at Sam, "Nothing to it Dad, a piece of cake."

"Heck," Sam said with a large grin of his own, "he wasn't even bucking."

"You're more than welcome to handle the rest, old man," Kade replied jokingly.

"Who are you calling old?" Sam responded, "It's not the years, it's the miles."

Kade unsaddled the sorrel horse and released him into the large pen with the others. Sam rode Pard up alongside, "Nice job, cowboy. Now I don't know about you, but I'm hungry."

"Yes, sir, you read my mind." Kade replied with an exhausted look.

Walking out of the round pen, Kade followed his dad, carrying the bronc saddle on his hip. Exiting the gate, he made a loud and sharp whistle which had Grace, now a full grown dog, running to his side and following.

* * *

Kade sat at the dinner table finishing his well earned supper. Grace was lying on the kitchen floor while Sam looked in the refrigerator.

"Why don't you run into town tomorrow and pick up some supplies?" Sam said closing the fridge door.

"By myself?" Kade asked, a touch surprised.

"No, take Grace with you," Sam replied.

Grace raised her head at the sound of her name, as Kade took his dirty plate to the kitchen sink.

"You know what I mean, Dad." Kade said.

"I think you can handle it," Sam said looking at Kade, "Besides, that will give me time to check the cows in the east pasture." Sam pulled some cash from his front pocket, "Five bucks ought to do it."

"Ahh…" Kade said, blushing, "why don't you just give me a couple dollars."

"That's only going to get us half of what we need. You'll have to make another trip in a couple of days," Sam replied. He noticed the complexion change in Kade's face and he knew had nothing to do with food but rather with who was behind the counter. "Well, I suppose that will cover us just fine," Sam handed Kade two dollars and stretched, "I'm gonna hit the hay."

"Good night, Dad." Kade said stuffing the money in his pocket.

"Night, son."

* * *

Kade thought he would get up early and surprise his dad by getting into town before the sun came up. Instead, Kade found him already on horseback next to the nearly two decade old pickup.

"You remember what we need, right?" Sam asked.

"Yes, sir," Kade replied with Grace at his side.

"Don't forget the coffee," Sam said.

Opening the driver's side door, Kade said with a shrug, "I got it, Dad." Grace jumped in the open door and sat on the bench seat.

Nodding his head, Sam said, "All right." He started to ride away, then turned and said over his shoulder, "Tell Sarah hello for me."

Kade was blushing as he closed the door and started the pickup. The truck drove out of the ranch yard as Sam headed for the east pasture.

Chapter 20

The streets of Sheridan were coming to life as Kade drove the truck into town. Main Street had expanded in the last eight years, adding new stores, a restaurant, and a grocery store. The Murray's were nothing if they weren't loyal. Even with the new establishments they continued to do their business at Howard's General Store.

The café was starting to fill up as Kade parked the pickup in front of the general store. He opens the door and stepped out.

Grace makes a move trying to follow, "No, you stay here," Kade said gesturing with his hand. Grace reluctantly lies back down on the bench seat. After closing the door, Kade checks his appearance in the driver side window.

He straightens his hat and checks his shirt collar. After testing his breath in his hand, he takes a deep breath and steps onto the sidewalk.

Sarah was behind the counter when Kade entered the general store. Being seventeen, her mother often let her mind the store on her own. Her big blue eyes complemented her now long strawberry blond hair. Kade noticed her at once and removed his hat.

"Good morning, Sarah," Kade said with a smile.

Pleased that Kade was entering the store, Sarah replied in kind, "Good morning, Kade."

"How are you today?" Kade asked.

"Just fine, how about yourself?" Sarah said.

"I am good doing," Kade said with confidence.

"What?" Sarah asked confused.

"I mean, I'm fine," Kade quickly corrected. He has known Sarah his whole life, but lately he can't seem to think clearly around her. Wanting to save face and change the subject, he asked, "George around?"

Sarah has always thought Kade's nervousness was cute, but she did not want to embarrass him. "If Red's truck is at the bar, George is usually there with him," she replied.

"At eight in the morning?" Kade asked.

"They like to get started early," Sarah replied.

"How is the Cowboy Deli doing?" Kade asked, keeping with the small talk.

Since the new grocery store opened, the Howards had to try new ways to bring in customers. They finally said 'yes' to George's repeated attempts to rent out one of their store rooms. A counter was added and a couple of booths and George's Cowboy Deli was established.

"If he was ever here, it would do a lot better." Sarah said, "I've gotten pretty good at making his sandwiches. I hate making the Red Burk."

"What's the Red Burk?" Kade replied, almost afraid to ask.

"It kind of creeps me out. Calf fries, sauerkraut and a little bit of mustard," Sarah replied with a shiver. "I don't have to make many of them; Red and George are the only ones who eat them."

"Well, it probably smells just like them," Kade said, now running out of things to talk about. "I need to get some supplies."

"Okay," Sarah said with a smile, "I'll be here if you need anything."

* * *

A brand new white Cadillac pulls up and parks right next to the Murray's old pickup truck. Lester, who tells everyone 'he's sixty eight years young,' shuts the car off and gets out. Standing, he spots Grace lying on the bench seat and he can't help but smile.

* * *

Sarah is ringing up Kade's purchases at the main counter. "Where's your dad?" she asked.

"He's at the ranch. He figured he could get more work done if I just went to town," Kade replied.

"Why so few purchases today?" Sarah asked, appalled she was sounding like her mother: nosey.

"Dad…didn't want to waste money letting fresh food go unused."

"I agree with your dad." Sarah said, "More trips wouldn't hurt at all. We have more books to go over. Have you been reading?"

"Yes…" Kade replied, shuffling his feet, "of course."

Sarah finished bagging the purchases. "Well, there you go. I guess I will be seeing you soon."

"Yeah, you will," Kade said with a half smile, "Goodbye."

"Bye," Sarah replied with a grin.

Exiting the general store, Kade stepped onto the sidewalk and headed for the pickup, heart beating hard. The only person in the world that could make him feel this way was

Sarah. He was quickly brought out of his trance by a voice from behind, "Kade, how are you?"

Kade turned around, "Oh," he said when he realized who the voice belonged to. "Hello, Mr. Morgan."

"How are things treating you, son?" Lester asked with enthusiasm, since Sam was nowhere to be seen.

"Fine," Kade replied, and then started for the pickup, "I'm sorry, Mr. Morgan. I'm in a bit of a hurry today."

Lester, enthusiasm drained, did not see the point in replying, it would be another losing battle. He watched Kade get in the truck, start it up, and drive away as he stood there with a disappointed look on his face.

***

Kade was driving down the main highway, deep in thought, with Grace sitting beside him. He hoped no one saw him talking with Lester. If it got back to his dad, it would be another 'talking to.' He thought he cut the conversation short enough while still being polite.

Through the windshield, up ahead, he saw a new Chevrolet pickup driving towards him, the driver with his hand out the window flagging him down. As Kade slowed the pickup to a stop, the Chevrolet stopped as well, driver windows next to each other.

Kade rolled down his window recognizing the driver, "Hello, Mr. Peterson. Is there a problem?"

"Oh, Kade, it's you," Paul said surprised, "I thought it was your dad. Sam finally letting you venture out on your own?"

"I don't know about that. I'm just coming from town," Kade replied.

"That's a start," Paul said, "Anyways, when you see your dad, tell him that I would like to have those horses by next week."

Kade nods his head, "Sure thing, Mr. Peterson."

"Thanks, Kade, I'll see you later." Paul said.

"Bye, Mr. Peterson." Kade said as he rolled his window back up. Kade continues down the road as Paul drives in the opposite direction.

Chapter 21

With the mid-morning sun on his back, Sam

rode the fence line in the east pasture. That

particular stretch of fence butted up against

one of the main roads. Something about the

time of day, the terrain, the bushes, the

fence line, and even the highway brought a

vivid memory rushing back. Sam's mind drifted

off, seventeen years prior.

* * *

Sam was drinking whiskey from a flask as

he rode the fence line. He was visibly drunk,

swaying in the saddle. As he and his young horse approached a group of bushes, small birds flew from the foliage. Sam's horse spooked and jumped to the right, being drunk, Sam was two steps behind and fell off. His horse, free of its rider, ran off.

He landed with a thud and rolled up against the barbed wire fence. He tried to get up, but his shirt was caught up in the barbed wire. He fusses, trying to free himself but to no avail. He makes a big move and gets to his unstable feet, ripping the back of his shirt wide open in the process.

"God damn no good horse," Sam mumbled as he looked around for his mount.

The sound of a car approaching on the road is heard and Sam turns around to face it. The car comes to a stop and Lester steps out of the driver's door. Upon seeing him, Sam drops his head and shakes it.

"Your wife said I would find you out here," Lester said.

Uneasy on his feet, Sam replied, "And?"

"Drunk as a skunk," Lester said, disgusted by the scene in front of him.

Sam stumbled to the fence line, "You got something to say, say it!"

Lester shook his head and looked Sam in his bloodshot eyes, "How the hell do you think you can take care of this place let alone a family? You can't even take care of yourself."

"Is that a fact?" Sam said.

"That's a fact," Lester replied.

"And you're so good at taking care of a family?" Sam retorted, "There are people who would disagree."

"I've made mistakes, yes," Lester said staring at Sam. "I'm just trying to help you from making the same."

"I don't want your help!" Sam shouted as he swayed, "Besides, you've never liked me! Hell you don't like anyone." Sam looked Lester right in the eye. "That's probably why your wife left you."

The remark catches Lester off guard and his temper flares. He walks up to the fence line and punches Sam square in the face, knocking him backwards. "You better watch your mouth, Sam Murray!" Lester shouted, "You have no idea what you're talking about!

"I hope you packed a lunch," Sam said, wiping blood from his nose, "'Cause I'm about to whip your ass up and down this road." Sam got back to his feet and charged the fence line. Lester took a step back and prepared for the altercation.

Suddenly Sam's new Ford pickup races to the fence line, screeching to a stop. Emmie jumps out of the driver's side and slams the door shut. "Stop it! Stop it now!" She yelled as she placed herself between Lester and Sam. Having the fence between her and Sam, the only option was to push Lester back towards his car. "Enough of this! You need to go home," she said to him.

"No!" Sam protested, "Let me finish this. I won't have him judging me!"

Emmie turned to Sam with a stern look, "I said enough, Sam. I will deal with you myself." As mad and drunk as he was, Sam stopped. There was something forceful in Emmie's gaze.

"Good luck with…" Lester interjected but was cut off.

"He is my husband. I appreciate your concern, but it is time for you to go," Emmie said, clearly in no mood to be questioned.

Lester threw his hands up in disgust and walked back to his car. Opening the door he looked at Sam and said, "You're so worried about being judged, you can't even see when someone has your family's best interest at heart." He entered his car and drove away.

Emmie turned to Sam and stared at him, he was a mess; bloodshot eyes, bloody nose, and a ripped shirt. Turning away from him she spotted his flask near a fence post. She knelt down and retrieved it. Sam noticed what she had found and made a move to grab it.

"I think you've had enough," Emmie said stepping back. "I do not approve of his methods, but he has a point."

"Go on, take his side." Sam said staring at Emmie, "It was only a matter of time anyhow."

Emmie paused and took a deep breath; she was tired of this bickering. "I'm pregnant."

Sam stood shocked and surprised, the whiskey quickly drained from his system. "Emmie...I..." he did not have the words.

"Fetch your horse, Sam." Emmie ordered, "Sober up and we can talk back at the house."

Emmie, holding the whiskey flask, turned and walked back to the pickup. Without looking at Sam, she got in and drove away. Sam, dumbfounded, stood there for a long minute. He picked up his hat and began looking for his horse.

***

Sam sat there looking at the familiar scene and shook his head. "You sure could make a point, honey." Looking at the sky, he whispered, "God I miss you."

"Good Morning," a voice said, Sam turned to face it. The fat bellied warden, who ran the chain gang, was riding his horse up the road. His uniform and mirrored sunglasses hadn't changed, which in turn made the warden look like he never aged.

"Well, hello, Warden," Sam said with a friendly grin. He looked down the road and saw the prison work gang maintaining the road. It was the same amount of men as always, which still included the two hard-nosed convicts, Charlie and Frank. "Keeping the riff raff busy again I see." Sam said.

"Yeah," the warden said looking at the men, "it's like herding cats." He started to pet on his horse, which Sam recognized. "This horse we got from you sure makes things easier. It's probably the best damn horse we've ever owned."

Sam always liked hearing positive feedback on the horses they sold. 'Word of mouth' kept folks coming back. "I'm glad he's working out for you."

"Say," the warden continued, "you got any more like him?"

"Hell yes. I have a whole pasture full of them." Sam said with a smile. "Are you looking for some more?"

"Yes, sir," the warden replied, "but let me get back to the prison and talk to the big boss."

"Just let me know," Sam said, "we'll get you fellers taken care of."

"Thanks, Sam," the warden said as he turned his horse back towards the chain gang. "I'll be seeing you."

"Take care." Sam replied as he urged his horse forward continuing to check the fence as he rode.

Chapter 22

Sam rode into the ranch yard just as the afternoon breeze started to rustle the trees. He saw Kade near the barn performing rope tricks like he was entertaining a crowd at Madison Square Garden. Grace was sunning her belly about ten feet away. The scene brought a smile to Sam's face.

"I bet you could give Montie Montana a run for his money." Sam said riding his horse up to the barn.

Kade, not knowing he was being watched, quickly stopped. His shyness and humble nature had gotten the better of him in his teenage years, as he shrugged his shoulders. "How was everything out in the east pasture, Dad?" Kade asked.

"Just the way it ought to be," Sam said getting down from his horse. "That fence you fixed, you did a good job."

"Thanks," Kade replied, as his dad led his horse into the barn.

Sam tied his mount to the hitch'n rail and started to unsaddle him, Kade walked up and lent a hand. "What's new in town?" Sam asked, "How's George's Cowboy Deli?"

"Sarah said he spends most of his time across the street with Red in the bar." Kade replied.

"Doesn't surprise me, those two have been joined at the hip for years now. I was hoping his deli would help out the Howards." Sam said.

"Sarah did say the sandwich named after you is the big seller, the one you told him mom made." Kade said.

"No kidding," Sam replied. "I'm gonna have to stop in and see ol' George. It sounds like he forgot where the work is. And how was Sarah?"

"She's fine," Kade said looking away from his father, "She wants me to study those books with her."

Sam nodded his head knowing that Kade's education was more than just this ranch. "Then we better get you back to town tomorrow."

"I ran into Mr. Peterson," Kade replied, trying to change the subject back to ranch business, "and he said he would take those horses next week."

Sam removed his saddle from his horse and carried it into the tack room. "Good," he said from inside, "We'll bring those horses in in the next couple of days."

Kade nods his head in agreement as he unties his father's horse and leads him to a stall. When he exited the barn, his Dad and Grace were waiting for him.

"Hey, son," Sam said, trying to tread lightly, "I know you don't want to talk about it. I just want to say I really like that Sarah." Kade exhaled and avoided his father's gaze. "Not only does she help you with your schooling, but she is as nice as she can be."

"Dad," Kade said blushing.

"We'll head into town tomorrow for your studies," Sam said, looking Kade in the eye. "Then we'll take care of those horses for Peterson." Sam put his arm around Kade and they walked to the ranch house, Grace following close behind.

***

Kade and Sarah sat at a table in the middle of one of the general store's stock rooms. Barbara had cleaned it out and added the table, a chalk-board, and a few maps. Not to mention a book shelf she kept stocked for study sessions.

Copies of *William Shakespeare's Henry the V* are spread out on the table in front Kade and Sarah.

"Kade, did you even read it?" Sarah asked, noticing the glazed over look in his eyes.

"Yes…Kind of…it's hard," Kade stuttered, "I don't understand what is being said. I thought you said it was in English?"

"It's English, old Shakespearean English." Sarah replied.

"Well, I think it's stupid." Kade said with frustration, "Why can't we just read Huck Finn again?"

"I've heard your dad tell you 'just because something's hard doesn't mean you give up'." Kade shot Sarah a look as if to say 'cheap move'. "Yes, the language is old, crazy, and hard to understand. That's why we're learning it. It's the language of love."

"Well," Kade blushed with the subtle hint, "I would rather be riding a good horse."

"That won't get you a diploma," Sarah said shaking her head. "Now, come on we can do this," she said, sliding her chair next to Kade and opening the book.

* * *

Sam stood in front of George's Cowboy Deli, as George, behind the counter made a sandwich. He was looking at the menu board and the two items that stood out to him were, *The*

Sam Murray Cowboy Deluxe and *The Red Burk*.
George and Red, the latter of whom was sitting
in a booth, had not changed a bit.

"Don't forget the red onion," Sam said
watching George work.

"No, sir," George replied wanting to
impress Sam.

"George, I hear things are going well,"
Sam said, and then turning to include Red. "If
you and Red can stay out of the bar. Singing
and…"

"Oh, he can carry a tune," Red chimed in
smiling from his booth, "it's just when he
unloads it is the problem."

"Hey," George argued, "I might not sing
well but I can dance."

"For someone with two left feet, you can.
Chicken's best at making those sandwiches
though,"

Sam took his bagged sandwich from George, "You might be right, and he might be a long lost cousin of yours, Red. You guys are two peas in a pod."

"The Burk family tree has only got a couple of branches," Red explained.

"Don't I know it," Sam replied with a raised eyebrow, "Thanks for the sandwich George, and do try and stay out of trouble." Sam exited the small deli, as George and Red went back to their bickering, and headed back for the main room.

Barbara was behind the main counter when Sam approached. "Hey Barb, I've come to fetch the school boy," Sam said, "How's it been going back there?"

"They've been at it for awhile now," Barbara replied.

"Shakespeare," Sam said shaking his head, "Kade was asking me about him. That's above my pay grade."

"It's been real nice you finding time for the two of them to study," Barbara said, "I think it's helping, at least I notice with Sarah. I swear she counts the days till their next study date."

"Don't tell Kade it's a date, you'll scare the boy off," Sam said as he and Barbara laughed.

Barbara pokes her head into the back study room, "Kade, your dad's here."

Kade, still with his look of frustration, comes through the door carrying his book as Sarah followed.

Sam noticed his son's demeanor and asked, "You guys getting it figured out?"

"Like a calf stuck in the mud," Kade muttered.

Sam laughed again, "How about you Sarah?"

"Slowly but surely, Mr. Murray, we'll get it," Sarah said with confidence.

"I have no doubt," Sam turned to Kade. "Come on, cowboy, we need to be getting home." Sam turned back to Barbara and Sarah, "Thanks again ladies, we will be seeing you."

"Thank you, Mrs. Howard. Thank you, Sarah." Kade said.

"No problem boys," Barbara responded, "have a safe drive home."

"Bye Mr. Murray. Kade, you read that book." Sarah said firmly.

Kade smiles and nods his head as his father exits the general store. Kade begins to follow but stops and turns around to face Sarah.

Barbara watched the young kids look at each other and decided it was time to make herself scarce. "I need to start inventory, Sarah I'll be in the back."

Once Barbara left, Kade got the courage he was looking for. "Seeing as how I will be back in a couple of days, do you think there would be any way," Kade was nervous and looking at his feet, "I could maybe take…only if you want…" He looked Sarah in the eye, "to lunch?"

Sarah smiled wanting to relieve Kade's tension, "That would be nice."

"Really?" Kade asked surprised.

"Yes," She responded, "I would love to."

"Great!" Kade replied with a large ear to ear smile, "I'll see you in a few days." Not wanting to ruin this perfect moment with more words, Kade turned and walked out of the general store.

Chapter 23

The sun crested the Big Horn Mountains, illuminating the Murray Ranch as Sam and Kade rode through one of their many pastures. Grace was trotting not too far behind. Both father and son were in good spirits. Kade didn't have to worry about books or saying the right thing to Sarah, today he and his dad were doing what they do best. Sam, enjoying the morning, had finances on his mind.

"With what we can get for these horses, we might be able to buy a new truck," Sam said, crunching the numbers in his head.

"I don't know," Kade replied, "I love that old truck."

"You'll love another," Sam remarked.

"Dad, I'm serious," Kade said, turning to his father. "I don't want things to change, even that old rusted Ford truck."

"I'm sorry, son," Sam replied taken aback by Kade's sudden insight into life. "I didn't mean to make fun of you. But change is part of life. The sooner you realize that, the better." Kade looked at his saddle horn as if he knew that. "Is there something on your mind?"

"I don't know," Kade said then paused; he knew what he wanted to say but didn't know how. "I've been thinking," he started, then just blurted it out, "I've been thinking a lot

207

about mom lately." Sam stopped his horse and Kade did the same. "I never got the chance to know her, talk to her. All I know about her is what you tell me. I feel she is connected to this ranch. If we start replacing things, I'll lose any connection I had to her."

"Son," Sam said looking at Kade with tears in his eyes, "your mom will always be on this ranch and part of your life. She was the best woman I ever knew. She's not in some old truck; she's in your heart. No, you never got to know her, but she smiles on you, everyday. Your mother will be with you wherever you go."

Father and son take a moment as each man lets their emotions run their course. Kade takes a deep breath as Sam wipes the tears from his eyes.

"She loves you very much," Sam said looking at Kade, "and so do I."

"Thanks, Dad, I love you too." Kade replied, feeling a weight lifted.

Sam nods his head and urges his horse forward. Kade, riding Pard, followed. Coming to a stop on the edge of a slightly steep and grassy slope, the pair overlooks a small herd of horses. Inside, Sam was happy Kade wanted to have a connection with his mother, and it was about time he helped do that. But for now, they had a job to do.

"Why don't you and Grace head over there and see if there are any hiding in the brush," Sam directed as he pointed to the right.

"Sounds good," Kade replied surveying the situation and pointing Pard in that direction.

"Listen," Sam said as Kade turned to face him, "if you come across that roan horse with the scar on his shoulder, do what you can to catch him. I'm tired of him always getting away."

"If I get a shot, I'll take it," Kade replied.

"Alright, but be careful," Sam said.

"You, too," Kade responded with a smile.

Kade rides down through the pasture with Grace following. It does not take the trio long to round up eight horses and start to move them back to the crest of the slope. Kade and Pard push the horses while Grace keeps them moving straight. With a whistle and a point from Kade, Grace will turn the horses left or right. Kade pulls rein and stops so as not to scatter the small herd, letting the horses graze while he waits for his father.

Suddenly, on the backside of the slope, thundering hooves can be heard. Kade turns just in time to see his Dad, on a dead run, chasing the roan horse. Sam has his rope out and is swinging a giant loop. Kade's face tenses as the roan horse starts to descend the hill, with his father not slowing down.

Sam throws his loop and makes a spectacular catch as the loose dirt churns around his horse. He quickly pulls the slack and gets one dally around his saddle horn. He starts to pull rein to stop, when his horse steps in a prairie dog hole. The fast pace of the chase had Sam's horse fall to his chest driving his nose into the ground. The momentum of the fall pulls the rope tight, yanking the roan horse backwards. The weight of the roan horse was too much for the rope and it snapped with a loud crack. The wild horse ran away as Sam and his mount rolled, end over end, down the slope, finally stopping and laying still.

"Dad!!" Kade screamed, watching the horrific scene unfold before him. He touched spurs to Pard and ran him to his father. "Dad!" he yelled again as he jumped off and knelt by his father's side. "Dad, are you alright?"

Sam lay next to his lifeless horse, knocked out. His face was covered in blood and dirt. Kade picked up his father's head and cradled it in his hands. "My God, Dad," he said with tears in his eyes, "Please be alright. You have to be alright."

Sam moans and slowly starts to come to. "Kade?" he muttered softly, looking up at his son, "What happened?"

"Your," Kade quickly replied thankful his father was awake, "your horse went down and you guys rolled down the hill." Kade looks at Sam's horse, lying dead from a broken neck. "Dad, just tell me what to do." Kade was having trouble catching his breath, "Please tell me what to do."

"Kade..." Sam said taking slow deep breaths, "I'm the one...who's hurt. You...have

212

to…keep a level…head." Sam paused and started to move his head, "Try and…help me…up." Kade slowly tried to help his father to his feet. But the injuries were too much and Sam let out a cry of pain. "My legs…broke…and" Sam said as Kade set him back down, "I think…my ribs…are, too."

"Dad, I have to get you back to the house." Kade said looking at his helpless father. "I'm gonna go get the truck." He laid his dad back in the grass, in the most comfortable position he could. He turned to Pard when his father let out another cry of pain that echoed through the pasture. "I can't leave you out here," Kade said to himself, surveying the situation, trying to think straight.

Where the small herd of horses was grazing, two large tree limbs laid in the grass. Kade turned to Sam, "hang tight, Dad. I

213

have another idea." He quickly runs over and picks up the downed tree limbs, putting each one under his arms. He dragged the large sticks over to Pard. "I need your help on this one, Pard. Dad needs your help."

Kade slipped the tree limbs through his stirrups and pulled them to his saddle horn, one on each side of Pard. He then tied them in place with his rope. Pulling out his pocket knife, he cut his dad's saddle off the dead horse. Placing a hand on the horse's neck, he paused a second to say 'goodbye.' He took what was left of Sam's rope and saddle blankets back over to Pard.

Kade looked over at his father, who was passing in and out of consciousness; he had to work faster. He quickly laid the saddle blankets across the end of the tree limbs and tied them in place. Standing up, he tugged on the makeshift gurney, to make sure it would hold. Satisfied with his work, he led Pard, dragging the gurney, over to where his father laid.

"Dad, I need to get you on this sled," Kade said kneeling by his father's side.

"I'm so tired, son," Sam said looking up at the sky. "When I close my eyes, I see your mom. She's smiling, pretty as ever." Sam talked as if Emmie was standing right there. "Son, she sees the man you've become. She's here for me. She wants me to tell you something; it's needed to be said for a long time. But I couldn't" Sam started to cry, and it wasn't from his injuries, "Lester…was her dad. He's your grandfather."

"What?!" Kade asked with what strength he had left. His whole world, everything he knew, trusted, and loved was falling down around him.

"Yes," Sam said closing his eyes in deep regret. "I never told you because when you were born, and your mom died...he took me to court...He didn't think I could raise you...I hated him for that." Kade starred at his father in disbelief. "In my heart I knew he did it because he loved you, he was afraid for you...he didn't trust me. I didn't care, I wanted to raise you myself...prove him wrong." Sam started to cough up blood, "Grudges are like poison, son...it kills the person carrying it. We both poisoned ourselves with selfishness and pride. My worst regret, I shorted you along the way. A boy needs his grandpa." Sam was having trouble keeping his eyes open as Kade cried. "Listen, the ranch is yours now, son...He will be there for you. He has always been there for you. I love you very much...tell him...I'm sorry."

Kade watched his father's eyes close, "No! Dad you're gonna make it! Don't go! Goddamn it!" He cried trying to convince himself. Scooping his hand behind his father's shoulders, he buried his face in Sam's neck, crying, "I need you." The tears rolled down Kade's face as Sam took his last breath.

Chapter 24

From the ranch yard it was a five mile

ride to where that particular herd of horses,

the ones Sam had picked out for the Petersons,

was pastured. There was good water from

streams that traveled from the distant

mountains but it was rougher country from the

rest of the property; not so flat with many

changes in elevation. Sam liked it for the

young horses to build muscle, climbing the

hills and slopes, learning where their feet

were.

There was no easy way to bring a herd in from this pasture, but Sam and Kade had done it before and knew the best route. The trail was not filled with the sounds of thirty horses, but the sound of one horse carefully making his way over the rough terrain.

Kade walked in front of Pard, his cheeks tearstained, guiding him on the safest path. Each step was planned out in Kade's mind, which was racing, full of questions and 'what if's.' He had to push those thoughts away and concentrate on the task at hand: they had to get his father home.

He sat with his father's head in his arms for a while after he passed. It could have been hours, Kade really had no idea. Time just stood still in that moment. Heartbroken, he got Sam's body on the makeshift gurney and tied him down, and started the long trek home.

As the sun descended, causing the ranch to be bathed in red, soft light; the horizon showed the shadowy outlines of Kade and Pard slowly dragging the gurney. Taking his beloved father to his mother's side, Grace faithfully alongside.

Arriving at his mother's grave, Kade collapsed to his knees in exhaustion. The sun had disappeared and a few stars had begun to dot the dark sky. Mustering the strength, he unstrapped his father from the gurney and lay him down next to Emmie's resting spot. He sits; looking at his Dad, knowing he's never coming back and he begins to sob again. Grace, visibly sad, goes to Kade's side and lies down, resting her head across his leg.

***

When the sun rose the next day, Kade woke up leaned up against the large tree. Grace was snuggled up right next to his hip; Pard grazing in the tall grass not far away. His family, as he liked to call them, had never left his side. A glance to his mother's grave showed that yesterday was not a bad dream. He wasn't done; he had to put his father to rest.

The next couple of hours were a haze, as he gathered tools and supplies in the barn. Taking boards from the shop, Kade put together a casket the best he could. He knew his father deserved better, but for now this would have to do. Loading the wood box and a shovel in the back of the truck he returned to the gravesite.

With Grace at his side, he finished the work of putting his father to rest. Again, time moved at a pace the Kade didn't understand, as if he was stuck in a moment as the world moved around him. He did his best to concentrate on what he was doing but his mind was filled with thousands of thoughts and questions. 'If only this and if I'd of done that' maybe his Dad would still be alive. But the one question that was front and center was 'Lester is my grandpa?'

Looking down at the fresh gravesite, he was almost surprised he had finished. His hands were filthy and blistered and his shirt was sweat stained. He set the shovel down and starred. The wind blew and some wild flowers caught his gaze, he could hear his father say 'why don't you grab some flowers for your mom.' He picked them and smiled for the first time.

"Well, Dad, you're home." Kade said standing in front of the gravesites. "Tell mom hello and that I love her." Kade starts to tear up, "I don't know how I'm going to get along without you." Kade falls to his knees, "I love you so much, Dad. I promise I will talk to Lester." He wipes the tears from his eyes and looked out upon the ranch. "But right now, there is work to be done. And nobody's gonna take this ranch from me…nobody."

Kade placed the wildflowers on both his mother's and father's graves. With a look of determination he stands up and walks away, Grace right at his side.

* * *

The rest of the day faded away as Kade just wandered around. His big speech about 'work to be done' was what he thought his Dad would want to hear. It also, for the time being, made him feel better to say it. But the truth was he felt lost, so many things to do and he had no idea where to start. He would have given anything for his Dad to walk out of the barn and say 'the works over here.'

Kade sat at the dinner table eating the supper he made. He wasn't really hungry but it was supper time and anything to make him feel normal was worth a try. He mostly stirred his food around, throwing chunks of it to Grace, who sat at his feet. After taking a few bites himself he got up and brought his plate to the kitchen sink.

He took a deep breath, as he tried to shake the feeling of loneliness. Nothing seemed to work, until he spotted a note his father had left on the refrigerator. *Petersons will be here to pick up horses on Tuesday.* Kade smiled for the second time, his Dad had told him were the work was.

He was done feeling sorry for himself. His father was gone, to treat him with the respect he deserved was to run the ranch the way he would. It was time to lift his head and keep moving forward. He turned to Grace, who was looking at him, "Better get some sleep girl, we got a big day ahead of us."

Chapter 25

The following morning the relative warm
waters of the nearby rivers and streams
generated a thick fog that blanketed the
Murray Ranch. The horses that were not
gathered the other day are bunched together,
drinking water at a creek. Some were fighting
for their turn as others waited. Yet all were
alerted, ears pricked forward, to something
moving through the fog.

Atop a hill, overlooking the herd, Kade
and Pard emerge through the fog coming into

view of the horses. The herd mills around at the sight of Kade, as Grace sits next to Pard. Nerves shot through the horses as their flight instinct took hold. Yet, before they could react, Kade descended the hill on the left and Grace, commanded by a whistle, approached from the right.

Within a few minutes Kade and Grace, on opposite sides, were circling the herd. The majority of the horses were bunched up together in the center of Kade's circle. He knew he was acting faster and more direct than his father would have liked, but being short-handed, this was the only way he figured it would work. If he and Pard had calmly tried to gather the herd and let them pick their way, they would be out here for hours, time that Kade could not waste.

Kade scanned the area for any horses they may have missed, about thirty yards away, behind a tree, was the roan horse with the scar. He still wore the broken rope of his father. Kade's jaw clenched and his first reaction was to pull his rope out and catch him. His father's accident was just that, an accident. But if he could catch this outlaw horse, finish what his Dad started, it might make him feel better.

His trance on the roan horse was broken when he noticed the herd was getting anxious at the sight of his rope. He and Grace had the horses fooled, thinking they were trapped, but if they made a break for it, they would be gone. He had to concentrate on the task at hand. He slowly put his rope away and turned his attention back to the herd. He thought to himself, 'another day; we'll meet another day.'

Kade whistled at Grace and she stopped and sat, opening a hole in the direction Kade wanted the herd to run. He and Pard pushed them forward and like sand escaping an hour glass the horses lined out and began to run. Another whistle commanded Grace and she immediately ran to the lead mare and stayed by her side. It felt different working the horses this way, without his dad, but Kade had to acknowledge, it was working.

With a whistle he could have Grace turn the herd any direction he wanted. This is exactly what he needed, no thinking just run as hard and as fast as you can and get this herd to the holding pens. He rode Pard like a jockey and pushed the herd as hard as they would run through the terrain of the ranch. Grace was like a bullet through the grass keeping them straight. The fast moving animals seemed to burn the fog off as they ran.

Kade had planned everything out in advance. He opened all the gates he needed on the way to the pasture. So when the thundering herd crested a hill and the arena came into view, the open gate brought the comfort of a job well done. He touched spurs to Pard adding more pressure to the herd urging them forward.

When the lead mare entered the large pen, Kade shouted, "Down, Grace!" The herd rushed into the arena behind the mare as Grace peeled off and stopped, panting from exhaustion. Kade quickly dismounted and dropped the latch on the gate. "Yeehaw!!" he yelled in triumph. Grace trotted over and laid at his feet, "Great job, girl, great job." Kade was petting Grace when Pard nudged him with his nose. "You, too, buddy." Kade said turning his attention to Pard, "I couldn't do it without you."

The trio stood outside the pole corral as Kade smiled admiring the herd they just brought in.

***

There was no down time after the morning's excitement. Kade had cut out the horses he felt Mr. Peterson would like. Other than his father being gone, nothing had changed; this ranch had a reputation to keep, he knew what he had to do. He grabbed the bronc gear and Pard, headed to the round pen.

Performing a two man job with only one still started out the same way. He chose his first mount, a big black horse, and roped him in the round pen. It took longer than he had wanted but he finally got the black saddled, with the help of Pard crowding him against the fence.

Now he and Pard led the horse in circles so the young gelding can feel the saddle. Like all the broncs before the black pulls back and jumps around. This is literally not Kade and Pard's first rodeo and they handle it with ease. After many circles of bringing the black gelding closer, Kade slips the halter on him and grabs the bronc rein.

"Here we go," Kade says a loud, out of habit. He tried to slide from Pard to the gelding but the black horse shied away. "Easy, take it easy," Kade said, reminding himself as well. The black horse settles down and Kade quickly slides across to the bronc saddle. Since no one is there to hold the bronc's head, Kade has to get ready much faster.

It does not take long for the black horse to realize he is free and he breaks in two. He dropped his head and kicked to the sky as Pard got out of the way. Kade was not completely ready so it took a few jumps for him to settle down and get his seat. The black horse almost bucked him off, hunching him down on his neck, but Kade dug deep and drove to the front end. From then on it was all business. No matter what the black gelding tried, Kade had the counter move.

Riding the black horse to a stop, Kade pet him on the neck and crawled off. Kade was filled with joy, he felt like himself again. He unsaddled the gelding and turned him out into the small side pen. Taking a deep breath he walked up to Pard, "You're my right hand, bud. I couldn't get this done without you." Then channeling his Dad he said with a smile, "We got four more."

***

Pard is in his stall in the barn as Kade poured him a large helping of grain. The hard working horse ate it with appreciation. Kade stood with his arms on the top rail watching, "I think we're gonna be just fine." This was the first time he had said such a thing and actually believed it. Grace rubbed on his leg for attention, "You, too, girl. We're all gonna be all right."

Kade exited the barn with Grace following. A spectacular sunset caught his eye and he stopped and stared. This was his first moment of enjoyment, besides working, that he had had since his Dad's accident. He took a deep breath and closed his eyes, "Dad, I did it." It felt good to say, and hear out loud. "I had a lot of help. Pard and I got a handful of them broke. I think Mr. Peterson will be pleased. Dad, I miss you…" Kade felt the feeling of self pity again, but stopped himself. "Today, out here working those horses, I felt you right by my side. You taught me well and you were right. This ranch will always be yours, mom's, and mine." Kade wiped some tears and continued, "What I'm trying to say, my family will always be with me. I love you both very much."

Kade stood for a few more minutes just admiring the sunset. He cleared his mind and just enjoyed the moment. When he thought it was time he turned and walked towards the ranch house, Grace followed.

Chapter 26

The large iron gate of the Wyoming State
Prison is illuminated by the head lights of
the prison chain gang bus. After an eight hour
day of maintaining the local roads, the
inmates are filing off the bus for their
evening chow. Their shackles could be heard
bouncing off the concrete path as they made
their way through the gate.

The warden leaned up against the granite
rock wall, counting prisoners on a paper list,
as they passed. The last inmate in line is

followed by a skinny guard carrying a rifle. He had a worried look on his face. Once the last prisoner entered the prison yard he turned to the warden, "We've got a problem." The warden stood up straight and the guard saw his reflection in the warden's mirrored sunglasses, which were intimidating enough in the daytime. The guard swallowed hard and continued, "We're missing two inmates."

The warden removed his sunglasses, much to the dismay of the guard, because his daunting stare was worse without them. "Who?" The warden grumbled.

"Charlie and Frank." The guard replied.

Crumpling his inmate list, the warden shouted, "God damn it!"

***

Throughout the night, Charlie and Frank traversed the terrain, taking paths only used by wildlife. They were not about to be picked up walking down one of the main highways. They still wore their prison jumpsuits and staying out of sight was imperative. Having worked these roads in the territory for well over twenty years, they each had a good mental map of the area.

Frank had been a resident of the state prison for twenty-five years. Charlie was incarcerated a couple years after Frank, and the two inmates became fast friends. They both grew up around Cheyenne and dabbled in armed robbery and grand theft. They had both laughed about how they only met each other after they were caught.

Good behavior got the two men issued to the work program, where they maintained the roads for the last two decades. After a while the guards started pairing the two cons together because their labor output increased working side by side. And that's the way it was for years.

Until last night, when Frank noticed, the young skinny guard had dropped his key. A quick nudge to Charlie had him pretending to adjust his boot, picking up the means to their freedom. They stood at the back of the line, next to the bus, and were counted. As the men were loaded, they ducked off behind the bus and dropped into a drainage ditch.

Crawling on their stomachs they entered a drain culvert that crossed under the main road. Removing their shackles with the newly found key, they listened and waited. Frank smiled when he heard the bus fire up and drive away. Charlie started to crawl out, but Frank stopped him, wanting to wait a couple more minutes. When the coast seemed clear the two cons made their way out of the culvert to a desolate and empty road.

Frank took the lead and the two men started to run. Since their fortunes had turned so fast, there was no real plan. They headed north, through the local ranches, making for Canada. They never stopped all night, never slowing to more than a jog. So when they crawled through the next countless barbed wire fence, they were beat.

The grass was tall and the terrain provided good cover, so they laid down to rest. The sun was just starting to come up, it was better to move at night, if they wanted to sleep, now was the time.

***

Kade was both nervous and excited when Paul drove into the ranch yard that afternoon. He wasn't ready to tell anyone about his father yet. He had just started to feel normal and having to re-tell the story did not set well with him. On the other hand he was anxious for Paul's reaction to the horses he had picked out and broke. It was a fine line, but he figured he could walk it.

Paul waved to Kade as he drove his truck and trailer to the small holding pen. He had been here enough to know where Sam wanted him to load horses. He backed his trailer up to the wood arena and slid open his trailer gate. He was a bit surprised no one was there to meet him and was about to walk to the house, when he heard the horses rumbling towards his trailer.

Turning in that direction, He saw Kade and Grace pushing the horses down the alley and into his trailer. Once again Kade impressed him, never having to be told what to do, just doing it. 'Sam should have raised my boys' Paul always thought to himself. He slid the trailer gate closed after the last horse entered.

"This sure is a nice bunch of horses." Paul said as he pushed his hat back on his head. "I wish your Dad was here so I could thank him in person."

Kade felt his heart drop as he stood next to the trailer. "I do too," he did not look Paul in the eye, "but he's here on the ranch." It wasn't a lie, in Kade's mind he was here on the ranch.

"Well," Paul said reaching into his front pants pocket, "Be sure to thank him for me. And thank you for loading these horses," Paul extends his hand, with the cash payment in it, to shake Kade's hand.

"No, Mr. Peterson, thank you," Kade said receiving the crisp folded bills.

"Please tell your Dad hello for me." Paul said walking over to his pickup truck.

"I'll be sure to do that. Good day to you, Mr. Peterson, and thanks again." Kade responded, thankful the conversation was over.

Grace sat at Kade's feet as Paul drove his rig out of the ranch yard. Kade waved and looked at the cash again, getting paid for a job well done always felt good.

***

The sounds from loading the horses for Paul had woke Charlie and Frank from their slumber. They came to slowly, then quickly looked around from their grass cover, making sure they had not been spotted. They had stopped and rested on a hill-top about four to five hundred yards away from the Murray Ranch yard. They saw, plain as day, Paul driving away and Kade standing with Grace.

"What now?" Charlie asked.

Frank looked at their prison attire, "We have to get rid of these jumpsuits." He said.

"What do you have in mind?" Charlie replied.

Frank watched Kade, the cash like a beacon in his hand, walk to the ranch house. "We wait for nightfall." He said as Charlie followed his gaze.

Chapter 27

Kade sat at the dinner table eating his supper. It was the second time he had to eat alone, but this time he was feeling pretty good. He had proven to himself that he could do it, he could handle the ranch. There were a thousand other things to do. Top of the list was, tell folks about his Dad's untimely passing and talk to Lester. But right now he wanted to savor this moment of accomplishment.

Grace was laying at Kade's feet hoping food would drop her way when suddenly she jumped up and started barking.

"What is it, girl?" Kade asked, confused. Grace had made her way to the kitchen door and continued to bark, trying to get out. Kade got up from the table and walked over to Grace, he peered out the kitchen window. "I think someone's out there." He squinted into the dark, catching movement in the shadows that seemed to be moving toward the house.

The porch light came on as Kade and Grace exited the kitchen. Grace took off down the steps and ahead of Kade barking into the night. As Kade made his way down the steps, the shadowy figure he saw, turned out to me a man dressed only in his underwear. The man was swaying and looked to be hurt. "Grace, down," Kade instructed, looking out for this stranger's safety.

"Thank you, thank you," Charlie muttered as Grace sat next to Kade.

"Mister, are you all right?" Kade asked concerned.

"Help me, please help me," Charlie said as he continued to walk towards Kade. "I got shanghaied back at the road, they took everything."

Kade's eyes got wide, "Good God, let me get you inside." Kade took a step to help Charlie and felt the crack of impact against the back of his head. Kade fell face first to the ground, knocked out. Frank stood behind Kade's fallen body holding a block of wood.

Grace turned and clamped her jaw around Frank's leg after Kade hit the ground.

"Get it off of me!" Frank screamed as Grace's teeth bit into his flesh.

Charlie kicked Grace square in the side, pitching her off Frank's leg. She hit the ground with a yelp and jumped right back up and back to the fight. Frank threw the block of wood at her head, knocking her out as well. Grace slumped to the ground with a whine.

"Hurry up and let's get him into the house," Frank demanded.

"What about the dog?" Charlie asked.

"Leave it," Frank spat, his eyes already turned toward the house. Frank grabbed Kade's arms as Charlie took his legs. They carried him inside and shut the door. A second later the porch light went off and the entire place was dark.

* * *

The morning sun beamed through the kitchen window landing on Kade's face. He had dried blood on his forehead and was tied to a chair. The ropes on his wrists and the sun in his eyes helped him come to. Blinking his eyes, trying to see straight, he saw Charlie and Frank stuffing their faces with food at the dinner table. Kade's blood boiled when he noticed they were wearing his father's clothes.

"Well," Frank said after a nudge from Charlie, who spotted Kade waking up. "It's about time you woke up."

"Let me go!" Kade yelled, pulling against his restraints. "Who are you?! What do you want?!"

Charlie and Frank both get up from the table. Frank stood in front of Kade. "Names aren't important kid. You just do what we say and you won't get hurt."

Kade's attention turned to Charlie, who was searching all the cabinets and slamming the doors. "There ain't a drop of whiskey in this whole house!" he shouted in frustration.

"Keep it down, God damn it…" Frank quickly replied but was interrupted by Grace barking outside. "Great! You woke the dog!" A quick glance out the kitchen window confirmed Grace running around the house barking. Knowing this could cause attention, Frank went back to Kade. "Now, kid, where are your folks?"

"They're," Kade blurted out but stopped; he took a deep breath and continued calmly, "They're out on the ranch."

Frank looked at Kade in disbelief, "I find that hard to believe with all the horses in the barn and the truck in the driveway." Kade avoided Frank's stare and said nothing. "If they are here," Frank explained, "we'll be waiting for 'em."

***

Lester sat alone at the café reading the newspaper, the main headline was the jail break, and drinking a cup of coffee. He had missed his cohorts for breakfast because he

249

had to open the hardware store early for Paul Peterson. He had a load of lumber Paul wanted as soon as possible to get started on a new barn. It was service like that that kept everyone coming back.

He was even able to hear about Kade through Paul. Paul had told Lester about the horses he had picked up two days ago. Even though the boy didn't know him, Lester felt pride when he heard people complimenting Kade.

"Hello? Mr. Morgan?" A voice called from behind Lester's newspaper.

Lowering the newspaper, Lester said, "Good morning, Sarah. What can I do for you?"

"Mr. Morgan," Sarah said with a touch of concern, "by chance are you going out to your ranch today?"

"I hadn't planned on it." Lester replied, curious about the request, "Why?"

"He hasn't come in." Sarah spat out, now visibly upset. "We had plans…kind of. Lunch, yesterday. He was supposed to be…"

"Who?" Lester asked confused.

"Kade," Sarah replied. Lester sat up and listened. "It could be nothing, Mr. Morgan. But Kade's always a man of his word. I just have a feeling something is wrong."

"Calm down, Sarah," Lester said, reminding himself to do the same. "I have been meaning to pick some things up for awhile. I'll head out there and check on my neighbors for you." Lester got up from the table, "Don't worry, I'm sure everything is alright. If you haven't heard from me in a couple hours, call Sheriff Steve."

Missing a lunch date for a rancher wasn't a big concern in Lester's eyes. But Sarah seemed worried enough, calling the Sheriff was really for his own safety. If Sam caught him nosing around, he would probably need the Sheriff to pull Sam off of him.

"Okay, let me get this right," Sarah said, "if I don't hear from you in two hours, call Sheriff Steve and send him out?"

"That's the plan." Lester replied with a nod.

"Thank you, Mr. Morgan." Sarah said as Lester threw some change on the table. Nervously Sarah watched Lester exit the café.

Chapter 28

About an hour later, Lester's white
Cadillac drove down a dirt road near the
Murray Ranch. Lester knew the best spots to
spy, for lack of a better word, on the ranch
without being seen. Stopping his car he
stepped out and peered towards the ranch
house. From his perspective, everything looked
okay, and nothing seemed out of place. Being
mid-morning, Sam and Kade were probably miles
from the ranch yard anyways.

Crouching down to re-enter his car, he heard the faint sound of Grace barking. He looked again, this time squinting his eyes, and vaguely saw Grace running around the house barking. 'That doesn't seem right' he thought to himself. Maybe Sarah's concerns are right or maybe they left the dog at home. Nosing around for such a trivial reason would most certainly end in a fight.

Lester was curious about the situation but he tempered his assumptions and re-entered his Cadillac. There were some things he wanted to pick up from his old barn, so he continued on his way. Perhaps by then he would get word or see that everything was just fine.

***

Exiting his old barn, Lester was filled with emotion. This old ranch, that he loved very much, always brought him joy, yet it also held many memories of deep regret. So much so he moved to town and could never bring himself to sell it. The old place was holding up just fine and he was proud of that. He probably hadn't been out here in over a year.

He was carrying an old saddle and Winchester rifle; both had belonged to his father. Tradition meant a lot to him and he wanted to display them in his store, show the tools of a cowboy from seventy years ago. Lester opened the trunk of his car and set the two items down. As he closed the trunk, a rose bush planted next to the barn caught his eye.

He walked over to the bush and pulled his pocket knife out. It was beautiful and always made him smile even though it was planted by his wife, who left this place more than two and a half decades ago. He cut two blooming rose buds off and walked back to his car.

Setting the flowers on the front seat, he made up his mind. Sam be damned, he was out here and he was going to see his daughter. It had been too long. He shut the car door and drove away from his barn.

* * *

Sarah was pacing nervously next to the main counter in the general store. She looked at the clock every minute checking the time. She knew the plan, but two hours just seemed to take too long. She picked up the phone, and then paused. 'Just wait for his call,' she thought. Like Lester said 'I'm sure everything is fine.'

She went to set the phone receiver down but again stopped. 'Being cautious never hurt anyone,' she thought and started dialing.

"Hello Sheriff, this Sarah Howard at the general store...I'm a little shaken up. I sent Mr. Morgan out to check on the Murray's," she paused, letting the Sheriff speak but his questions only amplified her concern. "Can you please just pick me up? I'll explain on the way," she injected. "Yes, I believe it's an emergency…Ok, that's fine, see you in five minutes."

Sarah hung up the phone and ran over to George's deli counter. "George, you have to watch the store. Something's going on at the Murray Ranch," Sarah nervously explained.

George stopped what he was doing at the sound of the Murray Ranch. "What's happening?" he asked concern evident in his voice.

"I'm not sure, and I don't have time to explain," Sarah replied over her shoulder as she quickly exited just as fast as she had entered.

George removed his white apron and jumped out from behind his deli counter. He exited the general store just in time to see Sarah entering the Sheriff's car. The flashing lights turned on as the car drove away.

Troubled by the situation, George spotted Red's beat up old truck in the saloon parking lot across the street.

The daylight illuminated the dark bar as George opened the saloon door. The patrons, including Red, sitting on a bar stool, had to squint their eyes at the brightness.

"Close the damn door, Chicken," Red blurted.

"Red, we got to go, something is going on at the Murray Ranch," George nervously spat out.

"Calm down. I've had a little too much to drink and I ain't due out there for two more weeks," Red drawled.

"The Sheriff and Sarah just headed that way with the flashers on," George explained.

Ten minutes later found Red and George slowly driving out of town. Having the Sheriff involved did make Red a touch nervous. Despite his outside demeanor, he cared for his friends. If something was going on, he was sure Sam could handle it. But George cared deeply for Sam and Kade and if driving him out there made him feel better, he would oblige.

"Can we go a little faster than thirty five? Something is going on out there and we need to hurry it up," George said anxiously.

Red turned and looked at George, "Chicken, how fast would you drive if you were drunk? You know, if it's not one thing it's another, and sometimes you wish for the other. What do you think about that?"

George just shook his head and replied, "Fair enough, Red."

* * *

Lester had parked his Cadillac on the road next to the fence line. He had snuck this way many times to see his beloved daughter. But like he had said, 'It's been a long

259

time…too long since I've seen you.' He carried the red roses for her.

As he approached the large tree that overlooked his daughter's gravesite, he was going over in his mind what he would say. But his train of thought was broken when he saw the fresh new gravesite next to Emmie's. Leaning down, he read the handmade wooden cross.

Lester's eyes got wide as he absorbed the black writing, *Sam Murray*. His heart sank, and he quickly turned and looked in the direction of the ranch house. Grace could still be heard barking, something was wrong. Lester laid the roses on Emmie's grave and ran back to his car.

Fearing the worst, he grabbed the Winchester from the trunk and had it by his side. With dusk arriving, he slowly drove down

the road, headlights off, in the direction of
the Murray Ranch yard.

Chapter 29

Kade was still tied to the chair when Charlie and Frank entered the kitchen.

"I'm tired of that damn dog barking," Frank insisted.

"I'll shut it up," Charlie replied. He turned towards Kade, "Is there a gun in this house, kid?" Kade said nothing and just stared at Charlie with hate in his eyes. The look threatened Charlie and he slapped Kade across the face. "Is there a gun, kid!?" he shouted.

"Knock it off, will you?" Frank said to Charlie.

"Fine," Charlie replied, picking up a kitchen knife. "There's more than one way to skin a cat."

"If you touch her, I'll kill you!" Kade shouted, bouncing the chair trying to pull against his restraints.

With an evil grin, obviously toying with Kade, Charlie opened the kitchen door. He quickly slammed it shut and looked at Frank, "Someone's coming!"

Running over to the kitchen window, Frank peered out, and saw the figure of Lester sneaking around the barn. "It's just an old man," Frank said as Charlie joined him at the window.

"Help me!" Kade shouted, hearing their conversation.

Charlie, dropped the knife, and ran over to Kade and punched him on the side of the head. "Shut your mouth!" he yelled as Kade crashed to the floor, unconscious.

"God damn it, Charlie, keep it down!" Frank said, still peering out the window. He was not concerned for Kade, he just didn't want to be caught. He was thinking fast now, "Listen, you go around back. If I can't get this old timer to leave, you bushwhack him from behind." Charlie nodded his head as he ducked out of the kitchen.

Lester was squatted near the barn, staying low. He had entered on foot, parking his car where it could not be seen. Crossing the ditch to the property, he came across the discarded prison jumpsuit and his concern grew. Lester carried the rifle low and out of sight until he knew what the hell was going on.

"Can I help you?" Frank asked as he stepped out onto the porch.

"Where's the boy?" Lester replied, his suspicions answered. "Where's Kade?"

"I think you have the wrong house, old timer," Frank said playing dumb.

"No," Lester said emerging from the side of the barn with the Winchester held high, "I think you have the wrong house!"

"Whoa!" Frank shouted surprised at the gun. "Take it easy, mister."

Lester cocked the lever action rifle and leveled at Frank. "What have you done with Kade!?"

Frank spotted Charlie sneaking up on Lester from the side, "Look, you just need to calm down," Frank said, trying to keep Lester's attention on him. "You have the wrong spread is all?"

Lester only had Kade's well being on his mind and this man's lying was getting in the way. "I'm not going to ask you…" Lester finally spotted Charlie out of the corner of his eye. He turned to face him as Charlie made his move. At the same time, Grace, not seen by anyone, attacked Charlie from behind.

Grace latched onto Charlie's right leg causing him to turn. In that instant Lester fired the rifle catching Charlie in the shoulder and throwing him to the ground. The report of the rifle scared Grace and she released Charlie's leg, going quickly to Lester's side.

"Get your hands up!" Lester shouted, re-cocking the rifle and pointing it at Frank. Frank hesitated, looking like he might try something stupid. "Now!!" Lester bellowed with authority. Frank quickly raised his hands high. "Now get over here by your partner."

Frank slowly walked over to Charlie, who was holding his bloody shoulder in pain. Lester covered them both with the rifle as the dark ranch yard was illuminated by the Sheriff's flashing blue and red lights. Frank dropped his head in disappointment as Sheriff Steve exited his car with his gun drawn.

"Les, what's going on?!" Steve asked anxiously.

"I'm not sure, but these two tried to jump me." Lester replied.

"Where's Kade?!" Sarah shouted as she jumped out of the Sheriff's car and tried to run up to Lester.

"Sarah, get back!" Steve yelled, wanting to get the situation under control. She stopped, clenching the skirt of her dress in her fists. Walking over to Lester, Steve recognized Charlie and Frank. "Well, hello boys. I will be damned. These two escaped prison a few days ago."

"Steve, if you got these two dirt bags covered, I want to check on the boy," Lester demanded.

Steve leveled his pistol at Charlie and Frank, "Yeah, I got 'em."

Lester ran to the front door of the house with Sarah right behind him. Opening the door, they enter with Grace sneaking in behind them. Their search ended quickly when both Lester and Sarah found Kade on the kitchen floor.

"Oh, my God…Kade!" Sarah screamed, seeing the dried blood on Kade's head, she feared the worse.

Lester set his rifle down and he and Sarah picked Kade up from the floor. "Son, are you alright?" he asked as he untied Kade from the chair.

"Yeah…" Kade replied, stretching and rolling his wrists. "But there are two…"

"Don't worry," Lester interrupted, "those coyotes have been taken care of."

Grace jumped in Kade's lap and licked his face as Sarah hugged him, "Are you really alright?" she asked, "Please say you're alright."

"I'll live," Kade said stopping Grace from licking him, "I'm alright, girl. I'm alright."

"Sarah," Lester said looking the house over, "why don't you get a wet rag and clean Kade's head wound?" Sarah nodded her head and went over to the kitchen sink.

***

Sheriff Steve had Charlie and Frank handcuffed and was placing them in the back of his squad car. "Watch your heads."

"I need a doctor." Charlie said wincing in pain.

"Sure, just as soon as I get you back to the prison," Steve explained with a wry grin. Frank just stared at his feet.

* * *

Kade sat in his father's chair in the living room, Grace at his feet, as Sarah cleaned his head wound. Lester sat on the edge of the couch, thinking as he watched.

"I don't know if I can ever thank you enough for what you've done." Kade said to Lester, turning he continued, "You, too, Sarah."

"I was worried sick about you," she replied.

"It's true," Lester said returning his mind to the conversation, "She came to me all concerned about you."

"Where is your…" Sarah started to ask.

"Sarah," Lester interjected, "would you excuse us for a moment?"

Sarah paused as if she had done something wrong, "Yeah, no problem." She set the wet rag down and started moving slowly toward the door. Glancing back at Kade over her shoulder she said, "I'll just be outside."

Lester waited for Sarah to exit through the kitchen door, and then turned to Kade. With a somber look he asked, "Kade, did those men kill your pa?"

"No," Kade replied, surprised. "What makes you say that?"

"I saw the grave, son," Lester explained with sorrow in his eyes and removing his hat.

Kade took a deep breath and lowered his head. He seemed to melt into the chair as he spoke, "His horse rolled down a hill. The fall crushed his chest, I…" Kade teared up as he relived the horrific scene, "I couldn't help him fast enough."

Lester exhaled and ran his fingers through his white hair, "It doesn't sound like there was much you could do." Lester paused to let the news sink in, "You've been out here all alone?"

"Yes, sir." Kade replied. He relived all he had been through in the last couple of days: bringing in the horses, breaking them, and not to mention being captured. But it was time to honor his father's dying wish. "Mr. Morgan…Lester. Before my father passed, he…he told me."

"Told you what, son?" Lester asked.

"You're my grandfather." Kade stated.

Lester is taken back and he began to tear up. "He did, did he?" He took a deep breath and continued, "I…I don't know what to say."

"My Dad's last words were for me to tell you…he's sorry." Kade said.

Lester had heard enough and the old cowboy began to cry. He leaned his weathered face into his palm, his elbow digging into his leg to support the weight of the emotion leaving the older man. Kade got up from the chair and walked over to him. Kade had just experienced loss for the first time; he knew his grandpa had endured more than one man should. They were the only family each had left. Lester looked up at Kade and the two men hugged.

* * *

After a short while Kade and Sarah, her hands folded into his, sat next to each other at the dinner table. Lester had made a pot of coffee and he sat across from sipping from a cup.

"After your mother died," Lester paused, thinking of Emmie, "I tried to take you from your dad."

"Take me?" Kade asked, "I don't understand? Why would you do that?"

"Your pa and I never really got along. Partly because I never thought he was good enough for your mom. But she loved him," Lester said, pausing to drink the coffee, "So I split my ranch and gave them this half for a wedding gift. When she died," Lester paused, "I blamed him. I didn't think he had it in him to raise you." He looked over at Kade and saw that this was hard to hear, "Pretty damn foolish, huh? God it's hard to imagine now. After the court hearing, I respected your Dad's wishes and stayed away. That's the reason I moved to town." Lester looked at Kade and Sarah, "You kids take a lesson from an old fool. Pride gets you nothing but lost time."

With that off his chest, he asked, "Son, how's the head?"

Kade felt his head wound, "It still hurts a bit. But this…" Kade took a deep breath, "this is a lot to take in." Kade turned to Sarah, "Sarah, did you know?"

"No," she said with confidence, "I think my mom had some sort of idea. But she never said one way or the other."

"Most folks respected your father's wishes." Lester added, "As time passed people just forgot."

Kade shook his head and looked down at the table, "Life took both my parents from me…" he lifted his head at looked at Lester, "but gave me a grandfather I never knew I had."

"I am truly sorry that your folks were taken from you." Lester said looking back at

Kade. "A child should never have to bury their father at such a young age."

"Mr. Morgan…Lester…" Kade asked, "can I call you grandpa?"

A smile came to Lester's face, "Nothing would make me happier."

"Grandpa," Kade said, liking the way the word felt, "I'd like to have a proper funeral for my Dad."

"I know you miss him," Lester replied seeing the hurt in Kade's eyes.

"Every day," Kade said squeezing Sarah's hand.

"Turns out, he was a good man." Lester said as he stood up from the table. "He needs to be celebrated by his family and friends." He walked over and stood in front of Kade and Sarah. "I'm moving back out here to be near you and make up for lost time. I've always loved it out here. It will all be yours when

I'm gone, but for now I just want to honor your Mom and Dad." Kade stood up to face Lester. "Be good stewards of this land. Keep raising their good horses and build memories with you." Kade gave Lester a big hug as Sarah smiled.

George and Red had finally arrived, and they were standing in the doorway, for who knows how long. "Well," George insisted, "you're gonna need some help."

Epilogue

Three months later things, had changed
but still felt the same. Lester had
transferred the deed to the Murray Ranch into
Kade's name. He also added to his will that
Kade would receive his ranch when he passed.
He never wanted the ranches sold, so having
them in Kade's name solidified the main
property would be whole again someday. He knew
Sam would be smiling down, because that meant
Kade would own a spread that would rival the
Peterson Ranch.

They had a funeral for Sam and laid him to rest with his family and friends, just like Kade wanted. It was not a somber affair, everyone from town was there and it was a celebration of Sam's life. George catered the event with his cowboy sandwiches. Red passed his whiskey around to anyone who wanted a pull.

Lester kept his promise and moved back to his ranch house. He and Kade worked the ranches as he had always hoped. Lester was standing next to the barn when Kade walked out leading Pard and handed the reins to him. Lester got on Pard as Kade walked back into the barn.

When he returned, he was leading the outlaw roan horse with the shoulder scar. The horse was outfitted with Sam's saddle. Kade swung up on his back and looked to the ranch house. Sarah, with Grace at her side, watched and waved from the porch. George sat on the steps eating a sandwich. Kade gave a wave and then turned to Lester.

"Grandpa," he said smiling and pointing, "the work's out there."

Made in the USA
Coppell, TX
27 July 2022